UNIVERSA

On a Yorkshire farm, a man is brutally ⸻ ⸻ solid gold bar.

A plucky young journalist sets out to uncover the truth surrounding the attack, connecting the dots between an amoral banker landlord, an iconoclastic columnist and a radical anarchist movement. She solves the mystery, but her viral long-read exposé raises more questions than it answers.

Universality is a twisty, slippery descent into the rhetoric of truth and power. Through a voyeuristic lens, it focuses in on words: what we say, how we say it and what we really mean. An addictively nasty celebration of the spectacular force of language, it dares you to look away.

13.03.2025

HB | 9780571389018 | £14.99
Export TPB | 9780571389025
Ebook | 9780571389049
Audio | 9780571389056

For publicity enquiries please contact
josh.smith@faber.co.uk

NATASHA BROWN

UNIVERSALITY

faber

First published in 2024
by Faber & Faber Limited
The Bindery, 51 Hatton Garden
London EC1N 8HN

Typeset by Faber & Faber Limited
Printed and bound by CPI Group (UK) Ltd, Croydon, CR0 4YY

A CIP record for this book
is available from the British Library

ISBN 978-0-571-38901-8

MIX
Paper | Supporting
responsible forestry
FSC® C171272

Printed and bound in the UK on FSC® certified paper in line with our continuing
commitment to ethical business practices, sustainability and the environment.
For further information see faber.co.uk/environmental-policy

2 4 6 8 10 9 7 5 3 1

AUTHOR'S NOTE

This book is a work of fiction. Any events, descriptions or statements concerning real persons or entities should not be considered factual or informational.

I, in fact, am the only fictional character in the book until I catch up with myself.

UNIVERSALITY

A FOOL'S GOLD

First Published in *Alazon* Magazine,
17 June 2021

A gold bar is deceptively heavy. Four hundred troy ounces, about 12.5 kilograms, of ultra-high-purity gold formed into an ingot – a sort of slender brick crossed with a pyramid. Holding one such bar on a chilly September evening last year, thirty-year-old Jake marvelled at its density; how the unyielding sides and edges felt awkward, yet somehow natural, in his hands. Behind him, from the main building of a West Yorkshire farm, music and coloured lights throbbed against the night sky. Roughly one hundred youngsters were partying in defiance of the British government's lockdown restrictions. Jake didn't look back towards the noise pumping from the farmhouse where he'd spent most of his fraught 2020. He wasn't even looking at the gold, not really.

The bar in Jake's possession was a 'London Good Delivery' – literally the gold standard of gold bullion – worth over half a million dollars. An obscene concept; Jake couldn't quite believe it was possible to hold so much 'value' within his two hands. Let alone to wield it. Again and again. Again. Until his target had finally stopped moving. But it had happened, hadn't it? Yes, it had happened. He couldn't stop

3

himself from staring at the proof. The motionless body lying at his feet.

At some point that night, or perhaps as daylight crept in at the edge of the horizon, Jake managed to stop looking and start thinking.

He decided to run.

In the weeks following Jake's disappearance, the Queensbury and Bradford local papers reported on the events of that night: an illegal rave, the resulting three hospitalisations, significant property damage and an ongoing police investigation. The story was soon forgotten, however, as national focus remained on the Covid-19 pandemic and the government's strategy heading into the challenging winter months. Yet unravelling the events leading to this strange and unsettling night is well worth the trouble; a modern parable lies beneath, exposing the fraying fabric of British society, worn thin by late capitalism's relentless abrasion. The missing gold bar is a connecting node – between an amoral banker, an iconoclastic columnist and a radical anarchist movement.

'Of course I want it back – it's my gold.'

Richard Spencer has not forgotten the events of that night. Indeed, as the legal owner of the farm, he thinks of little else. 'I want my life back,' he complains miserably.

The first time I meet Spencer, he sits across from me, his elbows propped against the dull aluminium top of our outdoor dining table. He chose the place – an earnestly ironic American-style diner in London's Covent Garden. The menu lists an £11.50 avo 'n' cream cheese bagel. Spencer wears a deep-blue Ted Baker shirt, starchy but unironed, with the sleeves rolled to mid-forearm, lending a disembodied, theatrical effect to his expressive hands and wrists. He's garrulous, keen to detail the many ways his life has been turned into 'an absolute shit show'.

An overly indulgent, even selfish, comment, perhaps. After all, since the pandemic swept across the globe in 2020, many people have suffered badly, losing their lives and loved ones. Spencer is alive and well. His loved ones are safe – though possibly not reciprocally loving, at this moment. But Spencer has lost something significant: his status. Back in 2019, all the excessive fruits of late capitalism were his. He owned multiple homes, farming land, investments and cars; he had a household staff; a pretty wife, plus a much younger girlfriend. As a high-powered stockbroker at a major investment bank, he enjoyed immense power, influence and wealth. He had everything. Now, stripped of all that, he has become the man across from me: a grounded giant, cut off from his castle in the sky.

Spencer's gold-thieving, beanstalk-chopping 'Jack' is Jake from the farm, whom he suspects of running off with the gold. 'Of course he bloody took it with him,' Spencer says, certain of his own version of events, despite having never met Jake.

In fact, Spencer knows virtually nothing about the man he blames for his ruin. Spencer invited Jake to the farm as 'a favour to Lenny', a woman he'd met in his building. 'Her friend needed a place to quarantine for a few days,' he says simply. Spencer doesn't know much about Lenny either. She was one of the few who remained in their Kensington apartment block during the lockdown, a time when most residents retreated to secondary homes. Does he know her surname? 'No.' Age? 'Um, mature.' Her flat number? 'I couldn't say for certain.' What did he actually know about this woman when he decided to hand her the keys to his farm? 'Well . . .' He hesitates. 'I knew her pretty well, in a sense . . .' He trails off.

Reluctantly, Spencer will admit to his philandering. He is separated from his wife, Claire, who remains in the family home raising their three-year-old daughter Rosie alone. 'Not exactly alone,' he's keen to point out. 'They have the nanny four days a week. And it's not like Claire has a job.' Claire and Spencer split in 2019 over his tryst with a colleague fifteen years his junior.

'Typical. He would say that.' Claire opens the large front door to her Cobham home one-handed when I stop by days later. A shyly curious toddler clings to her left arm.

We sit down at the kitchen table with a pot of filter coffee between us. Little Rosie lies on the soft-play mat in the corner, kitted out in stripy leggings, a builder's hard hat and a glittery tutu, mumbling as she forces plastic trucks to collide. 'I'm a designer,' Claire says. Since Rosie's birth in 2018, Claire has taken on part-time freelance work for a handful of clients. Before that, she worked at a boutique branding agency, after reading art history at Oxford, where she met Spencer. The pair married soon after graduation, spending a few years in London before moving to this exclusive village, favoured by footballers and financiers, and starting a family.

Claire is sanguine about their separation. 'People change, don't they?' Their house in Cobham never really felt like Spencer's home. 'He stayed in the city mostly. His hours were so long, it made sense.' In recent years, Spencer had begun spending weekends at his Kensington pied-à-terre too. 'I'm not stupid,' Claire says of the affairs. 'I know what goes on.' Still, it wasn't until Claire discovered the extent of Spencer's involvement with a younger colleague that she decided to officially call it quits. 'There's a line,' she says. Spencer had crossed it.

In 2015, Spencer's father died after a prolonged illness. 'That was the beginning of his farm obsession,' according to Claire. Every weekend Spencer would attend auctions or travel to remote towns to view land plots and properties. A late effort, perhaps triggered by grief, to emulate his father – a 'man's man' who built a successful construction company from the ground up. 'His dad never quite understood him,' Claire says. 'But Rich idolised the guy.' Eventually Spencer bought Alderton, an old hilltop farm in Queensbury, a quiet West Yorkshire village. Claire didn't think much of the property. 'It was a complete wreck. A rubbish heap on a big hill in an awful little town. No one with any sense would touch it.'

Claire's dismissal of the farm lands close to home. I grew up in Queensbury, a stone's throw from the farm. I walked past it almost daily as a child; occasional summer afternoons spent 'mucking in' with the Alderton family as a teenager were a part of my upbringing. Fresh produce was a staple at our dinner table. Nothing at the supermarket can beat the warm, frothy taste of unpasteurised cow's milk, ladled fresh from the milker's bucket. Though economically disadvantaged, and unapologetically working class, the town provided a wonderful backdrop to my childhood. It has value. But somehow, our country's towns and industries have become the playthings of London's elite. The Alderton farm fell on hard times in the wake of the 2008 financial crisis, when the government subsidies that had buoyed its modest revenues dried up. The livestock was sold off and the family boarded up the outbuildings. But living in the main house, without income from an operational farm, proved untenable. 'We lost everything,' Mrs Alderton tells me over the telephone. A gentle pain tremors in her voice. 'It'd been in our family for generations.' The Aldertons searched for new owners who would continue to run it as a community-minded farm, but there was little interest. 'We ended up selling to property developers. We had no choice.' No investment or redevelopment took place, however, though the farm changed hands a few more times. The abandoned plot remained untouched until 2016, when Richard Spencer snapped up the property at auction.

'He has a weird "prepper" fantasy. He thinks he can survive the end of the world there or something.' Claire is doubtful. 'I've never seen him do so much as water the garden.' Spencer went on to renovate the farm's main building, fashioning a refuge for when society inevitably collapsed – possibly galvanised by his part in the '08 crash, and the societal fragility each subsequent economic shockwave revealed. When a global catastrophe finally did arrive by way of a novel coronavirus, however, Spencer clung to London's familiar comforts: restaurants takeaways, his housekeeper and same-day deliveries from Mr Porter. He remained in his Kensington apartment, and the renovated farm stood empty.

Until Jake arrived.

There are currently no suspects in the police investigation. On the night of the rave, local police issued over thirty fixed penalty notices for lockdown breaches. As the venue owner, Spencer also received a £10,000 fine. Most attendees fled before police arrived, and interviews with the few arrested proved fruitless – the majority lived outside Queensbury and knew little of the farm. One unidentified person of interest was found unconscious and admitted to a local hospital, having suffered a blunt force trauma to his head. Two other attendees were treated for minor injuries. Initial news reports noted 'evidence of squatters at the property', along with an apparent 'small-scale marijuana-growing effort', which officers nipped in the bud, seizing everything. Spencer has been questioned, though police declined to provide details of his statement, citing an ongoing investigation. There is presently no search, however, for a missing gold bar – or Jake, for that matter. A police spokesperson gave a terse dismissal: 'Primarily this is a drugs offence, a serious lockdown breach and a potential assault. Not a wild goose chase for a pot of gold.'

Mixed metaphors aside, the investigation appears to have petered out. Until the hospitalised John Doe regains full consciousness, many of the goings-on at the farm will likely remain unknown. Today, the boundaries of the farm are still cordoned off by police tape, a striking reminder to the town's residents.

'I hate to see it come to this,' Mrs Alderton laments. 'Drugs, violence and who knows what else? That was our home.' The Aldertons believe Richard Spencer had an active role in the criminality. 'It's big business,' says Mr Alderton, a comment his wife relays to me enthusiastically. Spencer's months-long renovation of the farm's main house, which then stood empty, had already sparked speculation among local residents. 'Something's not right there,' Mrs Alderton surmised. 'Men like that don't spend their money for nothing.'

'I'm making a stock,' says historian and lecturer Rodger Walters, an explanation of sorts for the kitchen chaos surrounding him. A chicken carcass is splayed out in a Pyrex dish beside a large, propped-up cookbook and an impressive array of root vegetables, some half-chopped, others caked in mud. He directs me through the conservatory to a garden where his partner, columnist Miriam Leonard, sits with a tumbler of whisky, in spite of the biting cold.

It would not be unfair to say that Leonard, who goes by Lenny, exists in spite of pretty much everything. 'A rare dissenting voice in this perplexing time of media polarisation and moral orthodoxy, Leonard is one of the few souls brave enough to say the unsayable,' proclaimed the foreword to her 2018 book *No Mo' Woke*, a lightly edited selection of her newspaper columns spanning a twenty-plus-year career. Publishers, it seemed, had noticed that what Lenny said was actually quite sayable, and suspected it would also be rather profitable to print in book form. Lenny accepted a 'sizeable' advance in 2016 for a two-book deal, and began the work of repackaging her various columns into a single cohesive volume, her magnum opus, framed with an impassioned polemic detailing the imminent threat of 'woke culture and anti-white sentiment'.

'Problem is,' Lenny reflects, 'the book just didn't sell.' Apparently, the people who weren't embarrassed to place *No Mo' Woke* on their shelves didn't, by and large, actually have bookcases. Early indicators had been positive: the book garnered rave, collegial reviews from across the papers – *The Times* hailed it 'a breath of fresh air' and even the firmly left-wing *Guardian* managed cautious praise, albeit with a passing swipe at the 'unfortunate' title. 'Actually, the title was genius,' Lenny grins. She has a point. The title maximised upset and grievance, but was impossible to criticise without coming off as, well, woke. Even now, three years post-publication, #NoMoWoke remains a popular hashtag on social media.

Lenny's editor, Rob Neeson – 'a thirty-five-year-old with ridiculous glasses' – advised her to find a fresh take for the second book. 'Something "less Shriver, more Cohen" – that's what he actually said. Like I don't know how to write my own sodding column.' Lenny is entitled to some indignation. She's the seventeenth most influential columnist in the UK, according to the market research company YouGov. After punching her way out of the women's and lifestyle sections in the nineties, Lenny has established herself as a fixture in the opinion pages of Britain's right-leaning papers. Despite her oft-stated anti-social-media stance, in recent years Lenny has monitored Twitter fastidiously, always ready to pen a scorching opinion piece about the latest online brouhaha. She boils her sentences down to high-sucrose sweeties and calibrates her tone for maximum engagement. And newspaper editors know it: a piece of hers is guaranteed to attract clicks and social shares.

The book, however, was a reach for something grander. Lenny had grown disillusioned with her newspaper work. 'In the end,' she says, 'it felt cheap. I'd become an attack dog.' To Lenny, commentary should serve a higher purpose than mere punditry. 'We're not in the business of changing minds. I have to understand my readers' suspicions . . . their deepest fears. It's my job to inform those concerns by offering up the relevant *facts*.' She argues that her bruising brand of journalism helps readers to contextualise and interpret events. 'I zoom out,' she says, spreading her hands apart in demonstration, 'and reveal how all these trees come together as a forest.'

Back to those trees. Who is Jake, I ask Lenny. And how did he end up on Spencer's farm? I'd found Rodger simply enough from the electoral roll. He'd happily answered that he did, in fact, know a 'Lenny' when I called his extension at the university. But after a couple of hours' conversation with Lenny in the cold, I'm no closer to any answers about Jake or the farm. Instead of acknowledging my question, Lenny invites me inside for dinner. It's a generous interpretation of London's Tier 3 lockdown rules, but I accept, hopeful that the warmth, wine and food will encourage openness.

In November 2011, Indiya popped open a brand-new Quechua '2 Seconds' tent in London's Paternoster Square. In her rucksack she'd packed marker pens, baby wipes and a water-purifying straw, all in preparation to join the Occupy Wall Street protest. Barely nineteen years old, she'd accompanied her housemates from Central Saint Martins art school to join the ninety-nine per cent in an unprecedented uprising. 'It opened my eyes to the power of the people,' Indiya says of the experience. I find her sitting beside the now semi-conscious, semi-identified John Doe at the Bradford Royal Infirmary, the nearest hospital to the Alderton farm. 'His name is Pegasus,' Indiya says, reaching over the motionless man to rearrange his blankets, before smoothing his wayward hair. 'He's a visionary.'

Almost entirely unresponsive, Pegasus stares ahead with wide-open eyes. 'He's in a minimally conscious state,' Indiya says. 'It's a good sign – he's getting better.' Pegasus spent a worrying forty hours unconscious after police transported him to the hospital without identification. Claiming no knowledge of how Pegasus was injured, Indiya instead speaks of the 'chaos' as officers arrived at the farm. 'Everyone was running around, the music was so loud, it was impossible to know what was going on.' She spent days searching for Pegasus in the aftermath, before finally locating him here at the hospital.

Indiya is tall, six foot exactly, with mouse-brown hair styled in long dreadlocks, loosely tied back. Her organic-cotton face mask bobs as she speaks. Wearing an oversized waxed jacket with heavy boots, leggings and a cropped t-shirt that occasionally flashes her pale midriff, she looks like a revolutionary hippy from central casting. 'Occupy changed everything for me,' she says. She'd camped at the protest on and off for about three weeks, until her parents intervened: 'They only cared about me graduating, not, like, the large-scale inequality in the world.' To her parents' relief, Indiya did graduate in 2014, though she remained in close contact with the motley characters she'd met during the occupation, especially Pegasus. 'He's a magnetic force,' she says of her injured compatriot. 'He has this way of drawing people together.'

Though Indiya occasionally undertakes work in video game design, she's mostly rejected the traditional rat race, choosing instead to experiment with various communal living arrangements. Some were relatively formal, with leases or co-op agreements in place; others less so. 'I'm a hard-core Marxist,' she tells me solemnly. In the years since Occupy, she's committed to several other sociopolitical causes and is currently active within an Extinction Rebellion cell, a leaderless group of environmental activists who've staged political stunts and protests across the UK. 'Activism,' she explains, 'is crucial. It's now or never.'

In that spirit, Pegasus led a small group of activists to the Alderton farm last July. Together, they aimed to create a new 'self-sustaining community'. Christening themselves the Universalists, the group considered their takeover of the farm political activism, rather than squatting. 'It's an unused property,' Indiya says. 'There's so many buildings like that in the UK. All these spaces – empty. It's criminally wasteful, when so many people need homes.' The Universalists viewed the farm as an opportunity; it was a chance to realise their specific vision for communal living.

Today, that dream is officially over. After visiting hours, Indiya cycles the ten miles back to the farm. A heavy padlock and chain secure the doors to the main building, a charming two-storey stone house, punctuated with square lead windows, set atop a gently sloping hill. Bulging bin bags and a few suitcases are piled up out front, along with some mismatched furniture. There's a Billy bookcase, a couple of worn armchairs and what looks like the parts for a substantial sound system. Stray lengths of police tape flap about in the breeze as three young men load the bagged-up items into a small truck parked outside.

Indiya is disappointed. 'We were building something here,' she says in a wistful tone. Though only 'about a dozen' people lived full-time at the farm, Pegasus believed the Universalists were ready to expand. The main building was almost at capacity, Indiya says, but the group had plans to expand further by converting an outbuilding into functional accommodation. 'That night wasn't a rave – it was an open evening. We were opening our doors to potential new members, growing the movement.' Covid, it seems, was not a good enough reason to postpone such growth. 'The virus spread *because* of unbridled capitalism. Because of globalisation, and the profit-driven destruction of natural ecosystems. All this' – she gestures around at the sad aftermath – 'we were building the solution. Of course it couldn't wait!'

'Everyone pitches in. Everyone gets a say.' Indiya lists the rules of their burgeoning microsociety. 'Everyone is treated equally. We decide everything by a vote' – though Pegasus, as the group's de facto leader, held the power to adjudicate disagreements. This, Indiya insists, was an important improvement on her past commune experiences. 'Sometimes pure consensus isn't possible,' she says, 'and you just need a way to make a decision and move forwards.' As the community matures with time, the need for such ideological compromise would lessen, Indiya believes. Though she concedes that most of her other communal living experiments have ended before reaching such a point – either by fizzling out or collapsing spectacularly.

'But it was different here,' says Tim, 29, who had lived in a South London squat for two years before joining the Universalists. 'A farm offers possibilities that a city building just can't. We could have become self-sufficient here, living off the land, in conjunction with nature rather than against it.' Tim, who refuses to give his surname (citing his objections to 'the patriarchal concept'), wears tortoiseshell glasses and affects the mumbling grandiosity of a grad student. 'Humans are small-community nomadic animals,' he says, arguing that simpler models of living are needed to counter climate change and other pressing issues. 'We're not meant for living in densely populated areas, or eating tomatoes year-round,' he adds.

Although the Universalists had no formal hierarchy or fixed responsibilities, leaders began to emerge. Tim, who had previous experience with his parents' allotment, took charge of the farming effort. After sowing seeds late in the season, the group managed to grow a few vegetables. 'Kale, chard, sprouts – we even had carrots and turnips in the harvest,' recalls Tim. Despite his dominion over farming, he claims no involvement with the cannabis plants. 'Of course I'm not against it in theory,' he insists, explaining that the group's efforts were focused on establishing a sustainable food supply. 'We're serious about self-sufficiency. That's why we're doing this. It isn't a jolly.'

In fact, the Universalists eschewed many of the luxuries and conveniences Spencer had installed at the farm, mostly relying on the wood burner and solar panels. 'Humans need to get back in tune with the land,' explains Pete Wright, 38, a bicycle mechanic from Durham. With his manicured beard, neat chequered shirt and deep-blue jeans, Wright is the odd man out in this crowd. He looks positively conformist, aside from a messy topknot. More hipster than anarchist. But a few years back, when Pegasus chanced upon Wright's bike shop, the pair 'ended up talking for hours'.

To Wright, what Pegasus said made a lot of sense. 'He really got me. More than politics, or protesting, or any of that noise. He just understood exactly what I'd been thinking,' says Wright. 'He talked about how we could live differently' – outside of the forces of capitalism and consumerism. Or 'a bullshit-free life', as Wright calls it. Soon after meeting Pegasus, Wright gave up his cycle-shop job and moved into the same London squat as Tim.

'Quite the lifestyle change!' he laughs.

'You broke free, brother,' says the final Universalist, Rob Martin, approvingly. Describing Wright's encounter with Pegasus as an 'awakening', Martin is keen to share his anti-capitalist gospel further. 'Wage slavery. That's what the system thrives on. The credit crunch totally exposed it. Occupy was just the start. We're still carrying on that work.' Martin was a fifteen-year-old school student at the time of the 2011 protests. Undeterred by its underwhelming end, he makes an enthusiastic case for Occupy's enduring legacy: 'Bernie Sanders, Jeremy Corbyn, and obviously BLM. All of those movements came from what we started back then.' Martin has not had any first-hand experience with Black Lives Matter activism, explaining that he feels 'the environment is humanity's most pressing issue right now'. Still, he's sympathetic to many of BLM's stated aims, despite some concerns about the group's divisive rhetoric. 'Their demands are to the benefit of all of us, all humans,' he says. 'But focusing on race puts people off the message.

What we need now is unity.'

'That's why we're called the Universalists,' Martin goes on. 'We want change – we want progress – but for *everyone*.'

'We're open to everyone,' Indiya agrees. That said, the Universalists are a noticeably homogeneous group: young, middle class and white. 'This lifestyle takes a leap of faith,' she explains. Intentional living requires a step away from the 'activism myopia' that can ('Understandably!' she stresses) afflict marginalised groups. 'But we would welcome anyone with open arms,' she says. 'This is just the beginning. We'll get there.'

Once the last bag is loaded, Indiya leads the group to a large barn and forces the door open. Inside, the wooden ceiling is four or five metres high. Strips of dusty light stream through the gaps between slats. Remnants of stalls, feeding troughs and milking equipment line the walls, untouched by renovation. During the weekly 'community meetings' held in this barn, the Universalists debated all aspects of their fledgling community, from the group's mission statement to squabbles over the washing-up. Now, the four who remain have reconvened one last time to discuss an urgent problem: Jake.

When the group last met here, on the afternoon before the rave, they voted to expel Jake from their community. Pegasus informed Jake of the decision, telling him to leave by morning. There's confusion about exactly what happened next, as the gathering spiralled into a rambunctious party. Among the Universalists, the prevailing belief is that Jake, who took the news of his eviction badly, attacked Pegasus in a drunken rage.

'I would really like to see him face some restorative justice,' begins Tim. 'But as we don't have any way to achieve that, perhaps we should defer to the authorities.' Although the group initially refused to cooperate with the police investigation, Tim now proposes sharing information on Jake's whereabouts with police – an idea that's met with muted agreement. In the ensuing discussion, Jake is criticised for a plethora of misdeeds: shirking his work duties, growing the cannabis that landed the group in legal trouble and, most seriously, the assault on Pegasus. 'But,' Indiya interjects, choosing her words carefully, 'but Jake found this place for us. He invited us here. Even if he didn't become a constructive member of our community, that counts for something. Surely.'

'He nearly killed Pegasus!' Tim says, incensed. 'We all voted, we all agreed. Jake knew he was out. Fair's fair. But he chose violence . . . He ruined this for everyone.'

'That's unforgivable,' agrees Wright, speaking up for the first time. Looking down towards the hay-swept dirt floor and tapping his feet, Martin nods along. The group agrees to a vote. Even with only four people, it's a laborious process involving multiple rounds of hand gestures and slight adjustments to the mooted proposal. Eventually they reach a consensus: the Universalists will share their concerns about Jake's attack with police, without giving away his location.

After the meeting, Indiya walks along the perimeter of the farmhouse as the others return to the van. In her quasi-militant attire, she doesn't look wholly out of place trudging through the mud. Everything is packed away now, ready for the long drive back to London. Spencer's farm will sit unoccupied once again. At the back of the building Indiya pauses, looking down the hill towards the houses below.

'Jake hasn't been replying to my texts,' she says at last. 'I'm worried about him.' After another moment's hesitation, Indiya shows me an address on her phone. It's an E17 postcode, deep in London's East End. 'That's from years ago,' she tells me as I copy it down. 'Maybe it's no use anyway. But, well . . .' She kicks at a tuft of grass, then says simply: 'I don't know what else to do.' Disappointed by the majority decision to cooperate with police, Indiya hopes a restorative solution is still achievable. 'I know that's what Pegasus would want,' she says. 'I'm doing this for the greater good.'

A long the corridor leading into Ana Smith's ground-floor maisonette, there's a little wall of cardboard boxes. Each is neatly labelled: *Clothes*, *Electronics*, *Miscellaneous*, and so on. 'Jake's stuff' – Ana waves at it. She packed his things away after weeks of radio silence, though she's reluctant to throw anything out. 'I wouldn't feel right just dumping it.' She stares at the boxes, everything that's

22

left of Jake and their years together, while worrying a stray thread on her cardigan. 'Not that I expect him to come back,' she quickly adds. 'I know he's gone.'

Ana's home is in Leytonstone, East London. The house sits midway along a row of unassuming Victorian terraces, notable only in their bland uniformity. The small front gardens are grey, mostly paved or pebbled over. Each is blighted with a pair of green and black household bins, though Ana has livened hers up with a few shrubby plants and a hanging flower basket. It's an unlikely haunt for a revolutionary Universalist. 'I remember her,' Ana says of Jake's 'hippy friend'. A few years back, Indiya would regularly visit Jake while Ana was at work. 'They'd spend the day smoking and playing Mario Kart.' Eventually these visits stopped, though Ana claims not to know why. 'They probably fell out over something,' she says. Jake apparently had a way of getting into disagreements with his few friends.

What might Jake do with a stolen fortune, I ask. 'Nothing,' Ana answers with piercing post-break-up clarity. 'Money never held Jake back. He was his own worst enemy. He's probably driving himself crazy just looking at it, imagining all the stupid things he could do, and then doing absolutely fuck-all instead.' Jake left Ana in June 2020, after finding her newly constant presence in their three-room flat stifling. 'He was used to having the place to himself all day – doing goodness only knows what.' Jake hadn't held down a job since 2018, when he'd had a brief stint as a sales assistant with a nearby estate agent. During the first lockdown, he mostly vaped and played games on his phone. 'Basically, he lived here for free. I pay the mortgage and bills. I do all the shopping. All the cooking.' Ana shakes her head. 'All the cleaning,' she adds to the list. 'I know I'm an idiot.'

Though she knows nothing of the farm or where Jake has spent the last year, Ana isn't worried. Jake has a lifeline. 'He calls his mum when he's really stuck,' she says. Ana can't offer much detail about Jake's family, having never met any of his relatives over their three-year relationship. Family was a touchy subject for Jake. 'He's an only child like me,' Ana recalls. 'He never mentions his dad,' she goes on, though he would occasionally receive money from his mother. 'Weed money,' Ana clarifies, dismissively. 'That's all he spent it on.'

Ana had initially believed Jake's departure was temporary, a few days' separation to dial down tensions. 'All he took was his rucksack,' she says. But after weeks, and then months, stretched by without any contact, Ana was forced to accept that Jake wasn't coming back. 'It's a cowardly thing to do,' she says. Ana was left feeling abandoned at a terrifying juncture, when little was yet known about the virus. Her family, based in Cornwall, seemed a world away. 'It was very lonely,' she reflects. In the months since, however, resentment has given way to a wobbly sort of calm. Ana has reclaimed her home, clearing out Jake's things and making room for herself again. She's baked banana bread and sourdough and proved herself in the process. All that remains of Jake now sits in those archival boxes along the corridor.

'I suppose this is what you're here to see,' Ana says, taking the lid off *Clothing 2* and carefully unpacking the contents. It's what you might expect of Jake's wardrobe – knackered t-shirts and hoodies, an old pair of jeans. Each is neatly folded Marie Kondo style, though Ana admits that none of these items spark joy. 'Maybe I *should* dump the lot,' she muses. Poking around the other boxes, she eventually turns to the one labelled *Miscellaneous*. Inside, there's a fidget spinner, a few vape cartridges and a neatly rubber-banded stack of white envelopes. 'They're mostly phone bills,' Ana says, passing the bundle over to me. 'All his mail still comes here, of course.'

On the topmost envelope, bisected by the pale-pink band, a name and address are printed in an austere mono-spaced font. I pause to reread it. Then flick through the entire bundle.

'What is it?' Ana asks, confused.

Every letter bears the same name, undeniable in black and white.

It's Jake – or rather, Mr J. W. Leonard.

J ake Leonard. Miriam Leonard. Pure coincidence is too unlikely. With a nineteen-year age difference, the pair could feasibly be siblings – although, according to Ana,

Jake is an only child – or mother and son. The name is a concrete fact in the muddle of favours and liberties surrounding the Alderton farm. But it *is* just a name. Alone, it offers little insight into the most pressing question: where is Jake Leonard?

His options are limited. By all accounts, Jake is perennially strapped for cash, subsisting on the goodwill of others. Evicted by the Universalists, accused of a serious assault and separated from his girlfriend-benefactress, his situation is likely difficult. Even if Jake has the gold bar, as Spencer alleges, the practical alchemy of turning gold into cash is murky.

'We would need to authenticate that, yeah, absolutely,' Iain Stewart of Cash 4 Ur Gold explains. Pawnbrokers use an 'acid test' – a process that involves dripping an acidic solution onto a notch in the item – to verify the authenticity of gold. For larger bars such as Spencer's, additional testing may be required, which Jake would need to pay for himself. After all that, Jake can look forward to significantly less cash than the bar's actual worth. 'We wouldn't quote market value,' Stewart says. 'Gold in higher denominations is too illiquid. We'd struggle to sell the item ourselves.' In fact, even the prospect of holding on to the gold bar presents an unappealing risk. 'If it's too valuable, keeping it on the premises would be an insurance headache.'

Worse still, high-purity gold is actually quite soft; the surface of a bullion bar is easily scratched or dented. If Spencer's was indeed used as a bludgeon, it's likely now bent out of shape. The possibility of such damage provokes a disbelieving chuckle from Stewart. 'Yeah, we'd pass on that. Hard pass.' Jake would be better off selling to a specialist gold dealer, Stewart says. But without proper documentation for the bar – after all, it's allegedly stolen property – this would also prove difficult. Even if Jake has the gold bar, it's of little practical use to him.

What, then, is the purpose of owning such a cumbersome, high-risk item? For the price of that gold bar, a person could buy a home (even in London's outrageously overheated housing market), fund a lavish lifestyle for many years or make a significant charitable donation. Buying a golden paperweight is a comparatively pointless use of half a million dollars. Proponents of gold-hoarding argue that precious metals can offer insurance in the face of economic uncertainty. Growing distrust in banks and the broader financial system is driving many ordinary people to consider such alternatives. Cryptocurrencies like Bitcoin – electronic money that's sometimes referred to as 'digital gold' – are an increasingly popular anti-establishment financial instrument. But among older and wealthier sceptics, gold remains the preferred choice.

'Why does anyone buy anything?' Spencer retorts, incredulous, when asked about his purchase. 'I wanted it. I made enough money to buy it and so I bought it.' Mostly, he holds coins and smaller gold bars – 10-, 20- and 50-gram denominations – which he affectionately refers to as his 'biscuits'. Those, he explains, would allow him to barter or trade in the event of a total economic collapse. He keeps a handful in his London apartment, but most remain in a carefully fitted-out basement safe at his former home in Cobham. As a banker himself, Spencer is in a unique position to improve or reform his industry. Rather than taking action to increase people's trust in the economic system and ensure its longevity, he's chosen to hoard resources – guaranteeing his continued wealth in all eventualities. 'It's just smart thinking,' he says. 'Managing risks, that's what I do.'

His estranged wife sees the bar differently, as more of a trophy. 'He's very proud of it,' Claire tells me. Spencer bought the bar in 2017 as a fortieth birthday gift to himself. 'It took months of wrangling,' she says. Most accredited bullion vaults don't sell directly to the public. And even when high-net-worth individuals do purchase commodity gold, dealers recommend keeping the bars in managed storage facilities, rather than at home. But Spencer had insisted: 'He wanted it delivered right here.' Eventually, one dealer acquiesced.

'I'd actually forgotten about it,' Spencer says of leaving the gold bar at the farm. He'd placed it on the mantelpiece in the main building's living room, apparently unconcerned by the risk of burglary. Only when Bradford police showed Spencer pictures of the wreckage left after the Universalists' rave did he spot that his bar was gone. In retrospect, Spencer acknowledges that he should have kept a closer watch on such a valuable item, or at least have taken steps to secure it. Still, he's adamant that the lion's share of responsibility lies with Jake. 'Truly,' Spencer insists, 'I am the victim in all this. You mustn't lose sight of that.'

Most evenings, Rodger and Lenny eat late, sitting down at their solid-oak kitchen table around 8 p.m. Tonight is no different. Rodger places an oven-hot dish of shepherd's pie onto a trivet at the centre of the table as Lenny uncorks a dusty Malbec. The glass-ceilinged conservatory cloaks the scene in dark-night sky, twinkling with lights from distant tower blocks. The pair smile at one another, completely at ease in their own shared company. Like many couples, however, they found the conditions of lockdown strained their relationship.

'Lenny's mean when she drinks,' explains Rodger. Tensions between the two came to a head late in April of 2020. Feeling unsafe during an argument, Rodger locked himself into the first-floor bathroom and remained inside until morning. 'Lenny was at the door, screaming the whole time.' Rodger laughs about it now. But the next day his adult children (from a previous relationship) insisted: Lenny needed to leave. Fortunately, Rodger had access to a small flat – 'a bedsit really, it's a converted maintenance room,' he demurs – in a West London block. Rodger had initially purchased the modest property for his daughter's use; she'd lived there while pursuing a PhD at the nearby Imperial College

London. In recent years he has rented the room out cheaply, 'typically to older international students who want to avoid the communal halls'. Due to the pandemic-necessitated switch to remote teaching, the flat was unoccupied at the time, affording the couple some crucial distance to cool off.

'That's when I met Richard,' Lenny says. Believing themselves to be the only residents in the building, the unlikely pair became intimate. 'I was bored. It was sex, nothing more,' says Lenny. Her casual openness about the affair is striking, though Rodger claims not to feel betrayed. 'We were on a break,' he offers. His delivery doesn't quite match David Schwimmer's. Rodger shrugs and smiles. 'Things are good now,' he says.

'That's right,' Lenny laughs. 'Better than ever.'

Rodger stands to clear the table as Lenny relaxes into her chair. After nearly a decade together, they've settled into a comfortable domesticity. In here, Lenny does not seem to harden herself or her words. She's less guarded than when we first spoke. So, after Rodger leaves us to finish off some marking, I decide to broach the question of Jake once again.

If Jake is indeed Lenny's son, she certainly has good cause to conceal him. Her public persona is the opposite of maternal. In recent *Spectator* columns Lenny has repeatedly lamented the scourge of Britain's single mothers and 'bloody useless' parents. In 2013 she advocated for offering every woman in the UK a £799 cash payment to undergo 'voluntary sterilisation', a proposal that provoked outrage and glee in equal measure. Yet Jake is himself an underwhelming young man, hailing from the sort of 'broken' family Lenny frequently decries. Was he her hypocritical secret?

'It's no secret.' Lenny swirls the wine in her glass while speaking. In fact, she points out, she often mentioned her son in her earlier writing, those lifestyle pieces in the women's section. 'Did I become a mother when I was a bit too young? Yes. I'm hardly the first. I grew up working class and I had a kid young. So what? I worked hard. I earned a living. And I provided for my son. Don't lecture me with that puritanical middle-class snobbery.' Her criticisms, Lenny goes on, were aimed at the sort of mothers who refused to provide for their many children and instead relied on benefits – 'professional breeders', as she called them in a 2014 *Times* opinion piece. 'I'm the opposite of a hypocrite,' she says, topping up her glass. 'I know exactly what I'm talking about.'

Maintaining a child-free appearance now is simply a matter of branding, Lenny says. 'My readership is mostly males in the forty-plus age group. They don't want to hear from someone's mum when they read the weekend papers.' Besides, Lenny has other, more important topics to cover in her writing. 'My readers want banter, not babies. They want big ideas and insightful analysis,' she says. 'And that's exactly what I deliver. In spades.'

There's a formula to it, according to Lenny: pick something from the week's news and make a lofty comparison.

'Obscure elements of European history are best, but a Russian novel or philosophical theory can be just as effective.' Another route is to include data – 'accuracy doesn't matter much, just find a study and sprinkle a few of its percentages into the argument. Better yet, call up the study's author for an "expert" quote or two.' The idea is to bring each reader into the fold, she explains. 'Let him believe he's an intellectual, a real newspaper-reading man. Give him something to harp on about to his mates at the pub.' A mischievous smile flashes across Lenny's eyes. 'Even if he's only looking at screenshotted paragraphs on Twitter.' Her tone is light, but newspaper subscription costs have priced out key segments of Lenny's audience in recent years.

In Lenny's view, the harsh rhetoric of personal responsibility is not at odds with her own son's failures. 'There's a lack of opportunity for kids today,' she says. 'Jake is an unfortunate casualty of that wider trend.' She takes an iPhone from her pocket – comically militant in its bulky rubber case – and shows me a photograph of Spencer's 'so-called leadership team'. It's a group of five men and six women with a noticeably wide range of skin colours. 'These are the people he's given the top jobs to,' she says. They're all grinning, wearing charity-run t-shirts and holding up sloppy burgers or bottles of water. It looks like a parody of corporate diversity. 'Racial minorities are over-represented in this group compared to the UK population,' Lenny notes. She's sceptical of the bank's motivation. 'Do you really believe these are the most qualified people in Britain for the job?' she asks.

'These days everything is about race – everything. Woke capitalism is trampling all over the working class.' It's no wonder young people like Jake feel disheartened, Lenny argues. 'If you're a black disabled lesbian, or whatever, then you're hired. Regardless of qualifications.' Although Jake also lacks the qualifications needed for most careers, Lenny insists that's because the message to young people like him is crystal clear. 'Why bother? Of course working-class kids give up when all that matters is capital-D diversity. The deck is so clearly stacked against them.'

Efforts to increase inclusion based mainly on skin colour suffer from a narrow interpretation of diversity, arguably leading to today's censorious culture of groupthink. It's a problem that underpins Lenny's entire body of work, and perhaps even her life. Her blue-grey eyes turn mournful as she poses a crucial question: 'What happened to diversity of thought?' The words hang heavy in the air. Lenny tips and tilts her glass, watching the deep-red liquid settle into new equilibriums.

A wispy halo of hair surrounds Pegasus's wounded head. He reclines saintlike on a bed of two stacked mattresses topped with cushions. Lengths of silky fabric, their edges stapled to the ceiling, carve his corner out from the large, unstructured room he resides in, a former office floor. Now, instead of desks, printers and chairs, the space is cluttered with sleeping bags and improvised beds. Roughly thirty people squat in this disused community centre in Willesden, North-West London. Among their number are students, eco-warriors, musicians, Australians, and grizzled anarchists. Fluorescent ceiling lights illuminate Pegasus's languorous figure. A knowing smile plays across his lips. Indiya sits on the floor at his side, resting an elbow on the cushiony bed.

'We worked with soil, with music, with crops,' says Pegasus. 'And we were in talks to get some pigs, some little pigs and chickens.' Even after the farm's violent end and the weeks he spent in hospital, Pegasus remains nostalgic about the Universalists' vision. 'It was going to be beautiful,' he says.

Last week, Pegasus was discharged from the hospital as a free man, after police determined that the cannabis plants at the farm did not meet the 0.3 per cent THC threshold to be legally classified as marijuana. It is unclear whether the Universalists had intended to grow hemp – which is legal – or were saved by incompetence. Either way, no charges will be pressed. 'That's all behind us,' says a yawning Indiya.

Pegasus decamped to this squat for his convalescence. Posters and hand-drawn signs are taped to every wall. A fustiness permeates the space; think hot yoga studio with base notes of stale beer and cannabis – the acrid scent of revolution. As I take it all in, Indiya leaps up and lopes out of the room to help with cooking dinner. The squatters put on a communal daily meal, using the (sometimes literal) fruits of frequent dumpster-diving expeditions. There's a rota. Many of the residents here are self-proclaimed 'freegans', committed to eating only foraged and scavenged non-animal products. Scattered around the carpeted floor, however, are a few telltale polystyrene takeaway boxes along with empty beer cans and other trash.

Pegasus watches me intently, still smiling. 'What do you want to know?' he asks, eager to talk. His injury, sustained in the name of anti-capitalism, has granted him a degree of celebrity on London's squatter scene. Pegasus beams. 'I've had a lot of fist bumps. There's mad respect for what we did out there.' He's forthcoming, even jovial, about the details of his assault. 'Jake whacked me pretty hard,' he grins, touching a hand to a shaved and bandaged patch at the side of his head. According to Pegasus, Jake had indeed react-ed poorly to the news of his eviction. But the pair talked it out, coming to an uneasy truce. Once he'd calmed, Jake agreed to pack up his things and leave that night as request-ed. No hard feelings. He even suggested a walk around the grounds with Pegasus as a final goodbye. Despite the party's pounding music and chatter, it seemed peaceful out there, beneath the dampening night sky. Pegasus couldn't resist looking up at the stars – actual stars! Not the muddy dark-ness that hovers above London. All of it – the Universalists' whole experiment – could really work, he thought right then. After all, hadn't they just resolved a heated conflict amicably? 'I had this feeling,' Pegasus says. 'Everything was going to be okay.'

And then he hit the ground.

Jake, suddenly towering over Pegasus, was holding a shining golden brick up high. His face was manic and twisted with shadowy, exaggerated rage. He said something, but Pegasus couldn't make sense of the words. There was no more talk. Jake slammed the brick down, straight into Pegasus's skull.

'It looked like a fucking Toblerone. But it hit like a cricket bat.' Pegasus remembers nothing after that brutal first blow. Not passing out under the stars, or being taken to the hospital. What happened to the gold bar? Pegasus says he has no idea. The details of that night are murky. It's taken weeks for him to remember even this bare-bones account of events. 'Fair play to him – it's the best metaphor possible. A perfect example of how the capitalist system fucks us all. Anything pure gets destroyed.'

Incredibly, Pegasus harbours no ill will towards Jake. Instead, he points to the culpability of today's society: 'Humans are malleable,' he says. 'We are the products of our environment. Jake is just a symptom; the system is the cause.' He argues that anger and greed are not an inherent part of Jake's nature but rather 'the logical result of late-stage capitalism being forced onto a human being'. Pegasus says he experienced other modes of community while travelling abroad during his late twenties, backpacking, train-hopping, couch-surfing and passing through various off-the-grid communities. Inspiration for the Universalist movement struck much closer to home, however, during a ten-day silent meditation retreat Pegasus attended in Herefordshire back in 2018. 'I meditated for hours, waiting for my physical self to dissolve, and then I saw it,' he tells me. 'Like a vision. People from everywhere, overcoming all the barriers between and within, finding community. Real community.'

Drawing on Marxist ideology, B. F. Skinner-inspired behavioural science, and 'permaculture' ideals, Pegasus created a hodgepodge doctrine to underpin his vision. He's uploaded over twenty lengthy speeches to both SoundCloud and YouTube expounding the tenets of this philosophy. Opting out of 'the system' is, he insists, a form of political speech. 'We're demonstrating our objection to an economic and social system that amounts to fascism,' he says in one 2019 recording. 'All those people working every day don't even understand how pointless it all is . . . Their lives are completely pointless.'

'Most people don't like to hear that,' Pegasus explains to me now, in a more measured tone. 'But it's the truth. I don't know any other way to say it.'

Beyond symbolism, the gold bar itself is of little interest to Pegasus. 'We don't steal,' he says. 'Why would we? Property ownership is an illusion. Money is a myth.' For this reason, Pegasus is dismayed at the UK's intentional-living scene, where newcomers must typically cough up five- or six-figure sums to join an established community. Even such hippy-dippy cooperatives offend his radical concept of ownership. 'It doesn't make sense,' Pegasus says. 'If you're using the earth, if you're farming the soil, then you own it. That's that. Action is ownership. It isn't transferable. Or exclusive. You can't swap action for *money*. If you do that, it's just capitalism.' The payment structures some communities offer, allowing new members to join without paying the full amount up-front, incense Pegasus further. 'Congrats, you just reinvented the mortgage,' he snipes. The communard lifestyle should be accessible to everyone, he insists. 'That's what universality is all about,' he says, not for the first time.

Something like the Universalist movement was a long time coming. Pegasus had simply been waiting for the right catalyst. He's always believed he has what it takes to create a community from scratch. Even during his childhood he demonstrated a knack for attracting people. He grew up in Chelmsford, an affluent suburb in London's commuter belt, where at secondary school, he says, the teachers indulged him. One class tutor, he recalls, enthusiastically told his parents that Pegasus had 'a real shot at becoming the PM'. Although not the brightest student, Pegasus showed promise as a speaker and leader. During extracurricular activities such as the Young Enterprise scheme and the Duke of Edinburgh's Award, his aptitude for team-building shone. As an adult, however, he could never quite realise that early potential.

'I was lost for a long time,' Pegasus says, in a reflective turn. 'Trying to make sense of this life, it's mad.' He goes on: 'I don't claim to have all the answers' – a charge no one has made – 'but what I can do, what I've been placed on this earth to do, is shepherd others along the path of asking questions.' I ask how squatting fits into the picture. Pegasus bristles at the question, and more generally at how communities like his are portrayed. 'The word "squat" is a slur,' he says. 'It's rude and it's false. Actually, it's propaganda used by the media to scare people away from lifestyles that can free them.' Free them from what? He spits out the word: 'Capitalism!'

Presently, there's a ding. Pegasus pauses to look at his phone. 'Grub's up,' he grins, forgetting the previous moment's umbrage. With slow caution, he manoeuvres his legs over the edge of the low bed, then eases himself up into a standing position. It's still early days in his recovery. We join the shuffle of bodies out into the corridor and then upstairs. On this floor, a small former staff kitchen and its adjoining room have been transformed into a makeshift canteen. Alongside the standard kettle and microwave are two camping-style gas cookers, large chrome pots, pans, chopping boards – even chef's knives. Dishes, coated in dark grime, pile up in the sink, but the food smells undeniably appetising. The hungry throng makes its way over to a bubbling pot of stew, each person spooning their portion into improvised receptacles. Hanging back by the doorway, Pegasus watches.

'I used to get really excited by all this. People working together, feeding a community, all that good stuff. But it's actually fucking useless, isn't it?' he says, fiddling with a hand-rolled cigarette. 'Nothing is going to change.' He laughs. 'I guess I'm the jaded-activist cliché.'

Cliché or not, in a certain sense the Universalists can seem like a counterbalance to Spencer's excess. Both positions are undoubtedly extreme responses to the capitalist system: Spencer's embrace versus the Universalists' quixotic rejection. But Pegasus at least appears sincere in his desire to address society's problems, despite adopting dubious tactics. Lingering just outside the canteen, holding his unlit cigarette, he once again turns brooding. Why did the Universalist experiment fail so spectacularly? He has spent much of his recovery time considering this question.

'The world wasn't ready for it,' he says at last. Burned by the experience, Pegasus has no plans for a second attempt at turning his vision into a reality. 'I've done all I can. Someone else needs to pick up from where I left off. I hope they do.'

Jake Leonard's beard covers most of his cheeks, chin and neck. It's what I notice first when he answers the door. Then his clothes: a dressing gown loosely fastened over a stained vest and boxer shorts. His hair is greasy and unkempt, tied back into a short ponytail. The curtains are drawn and an energy-saving bulb washes the room in thin yellow light. There's a bed, wardrobe and desk, plus a lone Poäng armchair facing a television. In the corner, an open door points into a small washroom. A cramped 'kitchenette' (microwave, mini-fridge, electric hotplate) sits against the adjacent wall. It couldn't be further from the modern luxury of Spencer's apartment three floors above. Shoulders slouched in defeat amidst this pitiful tableau, a resigned Jake agrees to speak.

'My life is over anyway.'

Since the attack, Jake has been in hiding, camped out here in Rodger's Kensington flat. He wasn't certain that the place would be empty; he knew that Lenny, his mother, had been living here at one point – after all, that's why she'd sent him off to the farm. But he had no choice but to risk it. 'It's the only place I could think of to go,' Jake says.

In the confusion as police arrived at the Alderton farm, Jake managed to scramble into one of the vans heading back to London. Other revellers pushed in after him, keen to avoid an arrest or fine. As the door slammed shut, the van spluttered into movement. He'd made it out. 'No one knew me,' Jake says. 'And no one was really asking questions.' It was an uncomfortable ride, bumpy and tightly packed inside the dark, windowless van. Jake hugged his rucksack – weighty with its stolen cargo – and tried to figure out a next step.

His mind was ablaze with questions. Had he committed a murder? Had anyone seen what he'd done? How did police jurisdictions work – could the Yorkshire police arrest him if he made it back to the safety of London? Each time the van lurched to a stop, his stomach squelched and churned. It was more than drunkenness. Scenes of an ambush plagued him; he imagined officers ripping open the doors and dragging him away. Wiping at his cheeks, he tried to pull himself together. But it was useless: he was terrified. Any time he heard a phone notification, he figured that was it – he'd been found out. Hours later, when the van finally paused for a pit stop in Watford, Jake decided not to chance going any further with this crowd. On unsteady legs, he clambered out and scurried away.

After ditching his phone and SIM card in separate public waste bins (for fear of GPS tracking), Jake jumped the ticket barriers at the Watford train station and made his way across London to Rodger's flat. He's been here since, drinking, fretting and stewing over old quarrels from the farm. 'He was a megalomaniac!' Jake exclaims, still enraged by Pegasus's actions. 'He cut the electricity, he was planning to disconnect the water. He was trying to start a cult. It was self-defence.'

So why did Jake invite Pegasus to the farm in the first place? 'I didn't,' he says, flopping both arms in exasperation. 'I only invited Indiya. We were going to try farming, you know. Growing what we smoke and stuff.' To Jake's dismay, Indiya

42

arrived with a band of strangers in tow. 'They completely took over the place,' he says. Once again, Jake found himself trapped in lockdown, suffocated by the people around him. Tempers flared and accusations simmered to a boil.

Hunkering down in Rodger's bedsit for months without a phone, Jake was effectively cut off from the world. He watched the television news for any mentions of a murder in Yorkshire, but there was nothing. That didn't necessarily make him safe, he knew. Perhaps it simply wasn't a big enough story to make the national news. He didn't dare risk searching online; he'd watched enough crime shows to know that type of recklessness led to capture. His only outings were to the newsagent's – in a face mask and hoodie – for essential provisions. By the time I found him, Jake was questioning how much longer he could live like this. On learning that Pegasus is alive and (mostly) well, Jake collapses back into the armchair with a strangled gasp. 'I'm free,' he cries, shaking his head in amazement. 'I'm saved at last!'

Not quite. Although Pegasus has refused to give police a statement about the attack, a prosecution could still go ahead. And, I remind him, there's also the question of the stolen assault weapon – Spencer's gold bar. Jake leaps up, eager in his relief to accommodate any requests. Scrambling across the room, he opens up the wardrobe and shoves crumpled garments out of his way. He steps aside and there it is, swaddled in laundry. A real-life gold bar. It's dirty and scuffed, smaller than you might expect. But the ingot is undeniably impressive, simply as a physical embodiment of extreme wealth. And it's been here all along. Literally right beneath Spencer, who has spent oblivious months pacing just a few floors above.

Yet the revelation is curiously hollow. As Jake rambles on, giving an improbably convoluted justification for his 'inadvertent theft', the ingot seems to dim and dull, losing its lustre. In such modest surroundings it's rendered vaguely ridiculous. Perhaps the gold was only a 'MacGuffin', a meaningless object chased by Spencer that can offer no answers or resolution.

Jake looks down at the gold bar, the most valuable item he's ever possessed. Then shakes his head and scoffs.

'That fucking thing ruined my life.'

L enny writes on a late-2014 MacBook Pro in her airy home office. It's a warm May afternoon, two months after Jake Leonard turned himself in to the Metropolitan Police. The Crown Prosecution Service, responsible for bringing criminal prosecutions in the UK, has not yet made a determination in Jake's case. Lenny sits at an old wooden bureau, her body wound into a cursive G, tapping away. She's writing this week's column for the *Observer*, the *Guardian*'s Sunday paper and her unlikely new journalistic home – alongside Cohen, to her editor's delight. Her unshakeable focus brings to mind Mihaly Csikszentmihalyi's 'flow' or Cal Newport's 'deep work'. A rectangular pair of bifocals cling comically to her nose, just beneath the bridge. In this quiet moment, Lenny's appeal to a man like Spencer is clear: her self-assured competence is compelling. After another fifteen minutes or so, she's done. The printer begins to hum, lurching to life as Lenny closes her laptop. 'I hardly edit myself these days,' she says, looking the printed sheet over. 'I just write whatever I'm thinking.'

Despite her cavalier talk, Lenny's views are often nuanced and well considered; she doesn't lazily adhere to a single side for every debate. Take the issue of diversity in publishing: does Lenny suspect her book lost out to the recent glut of identity- and race-focused works? 'I actually love those books,' she says. Her smile is genuine. 'If people want to write amusing stories about their own debasement, and if those stories sell, why should I complain? Championing those books is, in fact, the very best advocacy for my worldview.' Far from complaining about tokenism or quotas, she instead offers encouragement to minority writers: 'More books like those, please.'

Still, Lenny retains her characteristic style: heavy on aphorisms, without wasting time with citations or justifications. She declares uncomfortably reasonable takes in a calm baritone. 'White men are the most discriminated-against group in this country,' she says. Explaining how a working-class white boy is less privileged than a wealthy black Oxford graduate, she ends on a populist note: 'Capitalism-fuelled affirmative action has gone too far.' Lenny questions whether a black banker would trade places with a poor white child – 'Of course not!' she answers herself emphatically.

A fair point, perhaps. But her rhetoric in past years was much more extreme. Does she stand by her previous columns and the book? 'Back then, I was looking at a symptom – overprivileged minorities – rather than the underlying cause, *classism*. Classism is what's wrong with our society, and it's so much more prevalent than racism. People are scared to admit that, but it's true. We need to fix it. Why are poor white children taught that they benefit from privilege? That's cruel and, worse, it's holding us back as a country.'

Her liaison with Spencer crystallised this mildly anti-capitalist critique. 'The guy is totally amoral – he doesn't care about this country. He doesn't care about British jobs for British people. All he wants is profit. If making a diversity hire means more profit, he'll gladly do it.' Though the details of Lenny's position differ from the *Observer*'s leader pages, her perspective has been met with sympathy at the paper. 'I'm home at last,' she says of her new column. It certainly seems so. Lenny's found common, fertile ground with her growing readership: Britain's exasperated middle-aged women. The sort who buy olive oil at Waitrose but can't quite stretch to doing their entire weekly shop on Ocado.

'*Observer* readers like blacks when they're starving in Africa, sure. They're interested in black "culture" – profiles of rappers; movies about addicts; books full of promiscuous women and struggling single mums.' But crucially, Lenny argues, her readers expect such people to exist in a separate social bubble. 'Would you want your child to lose out to an affirmative-action case? No – and neither would they. That's all it's about. The balance has tipped too far.' In a sense, Lenny is simply trying to level the playing field. 'My rhetoric in the past wasn't helpful, I can admit that. But my heart has always been in the right place.' A stack of old printouts lies on the desk between us. Lenny gathers up the pile, tapping the sheets into neat alignment. 'I'm writing sermons,' she says. And she means it.

'I'm proud of her,' Rodger confides. Not many people could evolve their worldview in the way Lenny has, he believes. 'It takes either a lot of empathy or, I guess, a personality disorder. I don't think there's any other way it can happen.'

Across her oeuvre, Lenny often returns to a fundamental question: who is our country for? London's wealthy, neo-liberal elites or everyday hard-working Brits? Her way of asking may be acerbic, but the question is crucial for a country seemingly stuck in an extended moment of flux. 'Brexit – which I'm no huge fan of, by the way – showed us that this country isn't working for its people. It was a warning,' Lenny says with uncharacteristic softness. 'We must heed that warning, and fix things. It's the only way to ensure Britain will survive to serve our children, and theirs.'

Inside Richard Spencer's dressing area, there's a lint roller, suit brush and valet stand with plushy velvet trimmings. With one soft touch, a drawer glides open, revealing rows of watches and twinkling cufflink pairs. Spencer selects a muted set of polished silver discs. He already wears a slate-grey Apple Watch. 'The little accents are what make a king,' he winks at me, paraphrasing Canadian entertainer Drake. In here, he enjoys the accoutrements of new royalty. Women of a bygone era had their finery – lavish gowns and jewellery – and Spencer has his armour of custom tailoring and expensive accessories. He opts for no tie.

'I'm ready to take my life back,' he says, ebullient.

Today he will return to his trading desk for the first time since his enforced departure, pending the outcome of the police investigation. Fully cleared of criminal wrongdoing, returning to his former life will now be trivial. 'Of course I haven't learned anything,' Spencer asserts, defiant. 'Other than fuck hippies,' he laughs as he makes his way out of the apartment. 'And don't buy property up north!' Police have not yet returned his gold bar, but Spencer is confident that he'll soon have that back, too. All is once again well in his world.

Despite the devastation visited on the Alderton farm and its local community, Spencer will face no consequences. Unlike Lenny, Pegasus and even Jake, Spencer has learned nothing from last year's debacle. It is no wonder that the financial services industry caused near-global economic collapse in 2008. In the cold light of 2021, Richard Spencer's conduct begs the question: why does our society tolerate these greedy, pitiful men?

EDMONTON

She had already, after agonising over whether to first wash it, awkwardly rinsed the chicken and then rubbed crushed fennel seeds and sea salt into its cold, dimpled skin. Next she stuffed it, holding the cavity open with her left hand and pushing in fresh oregano with her right. Six plum-sized organic tomatoes sat on a paper tray inside a clear plastic packet to the left of the chicken, still attached to the vine. After opening the packet and pulling each tomato from its short green stem, she sliced and arranged the watery segments around the chicken, sunny sides up. She wiped her fingers on a chequered kitchen towel and consulted the recipe on her phone. She dug two garlic cloves out of a bulb she kept on the spice rack, halved them (lengthwise, skin on) and dropped the four pieces in with the chicken and tomatoes. She took the solid butter from the fridge, peeled back the foiled wrapping paper and set it down on the chopping board. Carefully, she pressed into the butter with a dull knife until it met the unyielding surface beneath. Repeating the motion, she cut the smaller portion into soft chunks which she then duly distributed around the chicken, before pausing to clean her hands again with the towel. Emptying the oregano packet into a heap, she chopped the leaves roughly and sprinkled the pieces over the tray like confetti. With her phone, she took pictures of the chicken from different angles, first shooting from chest-height, then straining her arms above it for a top-down shot. Finally, she pulled open the preheated oven and slid the tray onto the middle rack.

By the time her guests arrived an hour later, the oregano chicken was slow-roasting; Hannah had changed outfit twice and reapplied her make-up once; the kitchen smelled sweet, golden-brown delicious.

'Are you certain, Hannah, that it's safe out there?'

Martin unclipped his helmet as he said this, clearly appalled. He looked at the dubious assortment of locks and chains along the left edge of the front door. 'I mean one-hundred-per-cent absolutely certain?'

'Oh, come on now.' Guin swatted him in playful reproach. 'You're obsessed with that thing!'

She swept along the short corridor, a whoosh of wispy hair and soft fabric, right through the kitchen and out onto the patio. It was a grassy little paved area just large enough for a picnic table and four folding chairs. Hannah had laid out a white tablecloth along with ramekins of nuts and olives and a bottle of organic wine from M&S.

'Isn't this lovely,' said Guin, indulgently.

Already seated at the table, John reached for the bottle and frowned at the label as Guin took the chair beside his.

'There's an app for that now, you know,' Martin said. 'No need to try and decipher the *runes*, as it were.' He sat down across from the couple and pulled his trouser leg out from his sock.

Sniffily, John inspected the bottle for a further few seconds, before handing it over to Martin. Hannah allowed herself a giddy moment of delight; she was glad, and frankly relieved, that this evening had come together as planned. Adult friendship bonds were tenuous; the past decade had been a lengthy demonstration of this truth. Owing to differences in circumstances and boroughs, these people – her shiny, sparkling friends – had drifted almost beyond her grasp. The article's success had been a lifeline, a reason to reopen communication. To check in and say *hi*, with the understanding that her overture would be welcome. Martin dramatically uncorked the wine and poured. Glasses clinked into Hannah's, a tinkling welcome back into the fold.

Her article, and its forthcoming television adaptation, was the first topic of conversation. After a few words of polite congratulations, Martin demanded details of what the producers would change.

'Well, it's going to be much more diverse . . . For starters, they're adding a love story between the hippy anarchist woman and the journalist.'

Guin raised an eyebrow at this.

'You mean between you and China, was it?'

'Indiya.'

'Did that really happen?'

'The characters are only loosely based on real people, remember. But anyway – no, it didn't, of course. I wouldn't get involved like that, I'm a journalist.'

'The consummate professional.'

Ignoring Martin's smirk, Hannah pressed on. 'And they're casting Jake as black.'

'There it is,' said John.

'What?'

He just shook his head.

'So what about Lenny,' Martin leered. 'Is she a *sista*?'

Guin snorted.

'Lenny won't be in it, actually. They're, well, we're probably changing Jake's mum to be Spencer's housekeeper, instead of just a neighbour. Kind of a composite character.'

'Oh, but that's quite a change, isn't it?' Guin frowned.

'I'm not sure how well Lenny would translate to the screen anyway.' Hannah spoke carefully. The adaptation, even as it took shape now, felt tentative and precious.

'In fairness, she was barely intelligible on the page – no offence. Obviously that's not down to your writing, Han. I know you like her, but . . . Lenny's a strange fish, isn't she? It's a bit difficult to find a coherent ideology across what she says.' Martin chuckled. 'Unless incoherence is her ideology.'

Martin had been tapped to interview Lenny in a few months' time, at a publicity event for her new book. After a quick google, he was left unimpressed: another ageing lady-populist braying for relevance. Hardly a rarity on Brit-ain's tiresome news media scene. Ordinarily, he would have declined the invitation, claiming a scheduling conflict, but he was keen to get in with this particular festival. He could pinch his nose and interview one silly woman, surely? Hannah was fiddling with the stem of her glass. It was unexpected – this little career revival of hers. To be honest, he'd written Hannah off years ago. Obviously not cut out for the trade. How, then, had she managed such a turnaround? He frowned as, oblivi-ous beside him, Hannah nosed at her wine.

'So why— No, Guinnie. It's worth asking. Why are you shoehorning identity politics into this? Why make this char-acter black? Jake is a real person. You do realise that? A *white* person, unless we're not allowed to say that now?'

'Broader appeal, I suppose,' offered Martin.

'Exactly,' said Hannah, keen to steer the conversation back to uncontentious, celebratory ground. 'The story speaks to a wider audience this way. The original piece was, I think we're still allowed to say it, John, very white.'

She laughed encouragingly, but John scowled on.

'It is set in bloody England.'

'Right, but a TV show needs to be international. If you want viewers, you need the *Fast and Furious* approach. Like it or not, people want some variety on their screens, especially for this type of thing. No, really. The production company analyses all of this. From the streaming data, I guess. I don't know. It's just not something they'd leave up to chance.

Besides, as a storyteller, I have to say it works, actually. It kind of resolves some of the inconsistencies in Jake's character. I don't know, it's hard to explain, but Jake just makes more sense, his struggles and arc feel more representative, when you know that he's *black*.'

Hannah tried to remember more of what her agent had said about the changes.

'It's like a modern-day *Bonfire of the Vanities*,' she added at last, 'unravelling the complexities of race, class and capitalistic greed in the social media age!'

John crossed his arms but said nothing.

'Well, congratulations. It all sounds very exciting.' Guin reached across the table and squeezed Hannah's hand. 'So. Is there another big investigation in the works? What's next for you?'

For the last few years, perhaps even longer, Hannah had not had a convincing answer to this question. Only that one summer between results day and the start of university had really ever afforded her an easy, agreeable answer. What was she doing now? It had been about a year since *Gold* came out. A life-changing year. The world, it seemed, had returned to something like normality. And her own life was perhaps also veering back on track.

Two years ago, she'd been falling apart. After being furloughed, her flatmate Fran had decided to move back in with family. As a freelancer, Hannah had no hope of furlough. She had no hope at all. Every financial assistance scheme announced seemed specifically designed to exclude her circumstances for one arcane reason or another.

Begrudgingly, her landlord had agreed to a thirty per cent reduction in rent, leaving Hannah on the hook for the remaining £1,337 each month, mercifully inclusive of council tax and utilities. Broadband was £40 per month, her phone contract was £12, and she paid £10 a month for Spotify. A tight budget of £25 a week would do for food, she told herself, and hit enter. Black sans-serif text in a little white cell announced the result: £65. She needed to earn £65 every working day. That was her personal cost of living. Reframing the month's total as a daily target made it seem more manageable, less hyperventilation-inducing; £65 wasn't really that much, was it? If she could land at least one commission each week, she'd survive.

But work had completely dried up. As a critic, with theatres shut and the flow of new books reduced to a trickle, there were precious few commissions, all fiercely competed for. And as for journalism? Suffice to say her pitches on BLM and anti-Asian hate were not enthusiastically welcomed by editors. Just another way, she smarted, that her working-class background disadvantaged her. She didn't have the *right* identity for identity politics (another idea tentatively pitched and firmly declined). Sixty-five pounds might just as well have been one million. She had no way of achieving it. Her stomach lurched as her overdraft swelled. Each direct debit was a blow to the chest. Every frivolous meal delivery, ASOS package and Starbucks latte she'd paid for over the years haunted her now. Her income had always been sporadic and unpredictable, true, but she could have saved more. Why hadn't she – and what would happen when her credit inevitably ran dry? Of course, she'd read about rent amnesties and paused evictions, but could that really work? For someone like her? She tried pitching a piece on it, but just putting the thought into words made her cry and shake.

'Come home,' her mother would say in that pleading, patronising tone. Every call was the same: familiar comfort quickly giving way to frustration as her parents begged her to leave London and move back to Bradford. Back to her depressing little childhood bedroom. Her depressing little life. A return was tantamount to complete failure. Her mum kept bringing up an open receptionist position at the local GP – as if it were Willy Wonka's golden ticket! Hannah exhaled, blowing away those stale frustrations. She pressed her laptop shut. A walk, in the right surroundings, could cure a lot. Her corner of the city couldn't quite offer beautiful landscapes. But a stroll along the high street would clear her mind.

Most places were closed: JD Sports, H&M, and all the charity shops. Boots was still open, along with a few of the cafes. She walked on, painfully aware that she could not afford to spare even a couple of pounds for a coffee and pastry. One sign stood out among the shuttered and unlit storefronts: *Nutraliving*. The name was spelled out in lime-green letters against a leaf-green background, but it was the taped-up note in the window that caught Hannah's attention. It read simply: *Help Needed (Enquire inside)*. Without really knowing what she was doing, Hannah stretched her mask from ear to ear and walked in. An older woman, reassuringly sensible in beige slacks and green apron, looked up from behind the till and crunched her eyes into a smile. A small, polite gesture that acknowledged, but didn't invite conversation.

'I saw the sign. In your window.' Hannah gave a slight nod towards the door. She was suddenly unsure of the mechanics of this interaction. She had never sought a job in person before. She didn't have a CV with her. Even if she had – nothing on it would remotely qualify her for this job. But the store manager, Martha, led the way, arranging an interview for later that day, after closing. Hannah accepted the job via text the next morning, and found herself working her first shift on the following Monday. The job paid £10.70 an hour. She worked nine-hour shifts five days a week, and earned the amount she needed to live.

The alien ease of a salaried income: every week! In her account! Working at the shop was so much less overwhelming, and less fraught, than freelance journalism. No more frantic scramble to survive. Mental peace darkened the fringes of her consciousness like damp. In the evenings, she couldn't bear to even look at books or watch television, so instead she left her music app on shuffle, letting the algorithm guide her, lying on the sofa and staring up at the spackled ceiling. Having never reviewed music, it still seemed possible for Hannah to actually enjoy it, without assessing, deconstructing, summarising.

An easy routine emerged: cheesy pasta or toast, orange squash, and an apple or some other piece of fruit for dinner. Then she'd turn on the music. It was like nothing she'd heard before: electronic highs and choral lows, an orchestral soundscape – beautiful, artificial – and the earnestly affecting lyrics, their simplicity. Utterly without subtext. Resistant to any analysis. Sunset on a phone screen, more vivid, higher resolution than life. Perhaps the dreaded algorithm wasn't so bad, if it could produce such music. Why had she been so set against it? Why had she ever been angry? In those moments, she could appreciate the unremarkable lives of her parents. She had (perhaps subconsciously) scorned the simplicity of their working lives, wondering how they could be content with so little from the world. But during those glacial evenings, lying on the sofa, Hannah finally understood the value of such a life.

Mornings: toast again or cereal, then a brisk walk to the store. Her horizon was blissfully shallow, with no more than the next hour or so of life in her line of vision. It was work she could do; straightforward tasks with reasonable time constraints and predictable outcomes. There was no vitriolic comments section beneath the shelves of healthful foods. No last-minute commissions rolling in on a Friday night, due first thing Monday and paying less (when you masochistically worked it all out) than the minimum wage. Best of all: no square-bracketed all-caps intrusions into her day demanding urgent edits on already-accepted-but-not-yet-paid-for work.

A shopgirl. Was this the person Hannah wanted to be? No, not at all. It didn't seem fair that she should have to give up her hard-won cultural capital for financial security. Be a journalist and live in poverty or give up your voice and earn enough to make ends meet. How was that ultimatum *fair*? She shouldn't need to choose one or the other; society was broken, she thought bitterly. So much hinged on accidents of birth, privilege rather than merit, what your parents could give you, rather than what you yourself could do – no, it wasn't fair at all. She ruminated as she scanned cashews (milked, buttered and whole), homeopathic remedies, gluten-free bread and pasta, egg alternatives, blocks of smoked tofu, natural deodorant, and plastic bottles of vegi-capsule supplements. She placed each item into doubled-up paper bags. She accepted contactless payments, offered email receipts, slid the packed bags over the counter and watched each customer carry their purchases away. Blissful weeks and months passed. She crawled back out of her overdraft.

In all that time – nothing from Guin and John, or Martin. No just-checking-in texts, no Zoom quiz invites. Nothing about the wedding either. A small outdoor ceremony; she'd scrutinised the careless, effortlessly gorgeous photo 'carousels' Guin posted to Instagram. Guests were limited, she knew. But still. Still. They'd invited *Martin*. Admittedly, her own relationship with the couple was strained by then. In

63

recent years, differences in wealth had become insurmountable challenges, unavoidably affecting Hannah's friendships. What had once been a kind of 'bohemian brokeness' indulged by her friends now seemed an unattractive, immature trait in this new phase of adulthood. It made things awkward. She had turned down an invitation to Greece, then Fringe, then Italy. She simply couldn't afford to join. At the few events she did attend, Hannah grumbled and kept a mental running total of the terrifying bill, always on the verge of barking her judgemental little laugh. Eventually the invitations stopped. No surprise there. And without that structural support, everything else fell away.

Dimly, faint and unacknowledged, Hannah understood that *this was it*. She was drifting away from the established social strata and into absence. A return to the undistinguished class of people the news happened to, not the people who made the news or, at the very least, commented on it. Back to the world of her parents. It would mean losing her voice, her importance and, she was embarrassed to admit it but yes, also, losing her friends. Even once she could afford to travel again, how could she, in all seriousness, expect to join Guin and John as the new sort of person she was becoming? What would their wider social circle, the stylishly semi-idle, make of such a 'job'?

They seemed beyond work, in a vaguely aristocratic way. The mundanities of jobs and salaries and bills were completely antithetical to her imagining of Guin's life. Working in a shop was not a possibility in that world. Confusion, more than even snobbery, she imagined, would be the response. The life of the starving artist had a certain romanticism. But to join the working masses? Well. At least for a little while, she determined to put such questions aside. For years, she had been struggling to maintain her foothold in their merciless world. Now she could finally allow herself to relax. The sensation was unfamiliar and warm, like the half-memory of pissing in a dream.

She signed out of her socials, then uninstalled the apps. Barely bothered to read her emails – what was the point? No commissions came her way. And she was so, so tired of watching people's lives from afar. Watching the world turn and evolve as she herself faded away. It was easier not to look.

And then –

From: itslenny@aol.com
Subject: A golden opportunity

The notification popped onto Hannah's screen and she tapped it. Of course she tapped it! That hard-wired dopamine-spiking habit was impossible to resist. Two days later, she'd quit Nutraliving. She was on the train back to Bradford. No, not the dreaded retreat: she was on a mission. The decision was easy; it was only a decision in the way that grabbing hold of a lifeboat with your last dregs of strength after bobbing hopelessly, desperately, in cold water was a decision.

And hadn't it all paid off? Her life now – totally transformed. Her friends, those glossy gilded people, welcoming her once again.

What allowed some people to 'make it' while others faded away, as Hannah herself almost had? She knew it wasn't a matter of hard work; she couldn't have tried any harder than she did those last few years. Luck was a possible answer, but it seemed too callously random. Increasingly, Hannah felt another, truer word burning in her throat: class. The invisible privilege that everyone tried to pretend didn't exist, but – it did. Hannah knew it did. She recognised it, and saw its grubby stains all over her own life.

Even now, she felt it keenly. A single question could still unravel her. She tried to return Guin's smile.

'Me? Oh, the same old stuff, really. I've got a few pieces underway, but nothing too exciting.'

Martin laughed. 'Playing coy, eh?'

He topped up Hannah's glass, then John's, after Guin hovered a delicate hand above hers. He emptied the rest of the bottle into his own.

Sipping his wine, Martin strained and cracked his neck while taking in the view – the backs and sides of all the rows of houses surrounding them.

'Edmonton,' he said eventually, exaggerating each syllable. Martin had lively eyes in his bland face, with two or three days' stubble shading his chin and jaw. He was tall and broad and enjoyed taking up space, extending his legs and arms and slouching into his seat. 'Why here? It's a strange neck of the woods to put down roots.'

'I picked where I could afford.'

Guin's mouth twisted, as if at the vulgarity of such an admission.

Hannah stiffened. 'Perhaps one day I'll join you all in Clapham.'

'Balham, really,' Guin said. 'We're just on the cusp.'

'Dar-ling,' Martin simpered, 'it's Clapham, always round up. Anyway, isn't it odd that all these areas of London develop their own mini-reputations. Who decides where Clapham ends and Balham begins? I don't know how anyone can keep track.'

'Crime rates,' said John. 'That's one differentiator. It is worth keeping an eye on those.'

'But it's not as if criminals can't get on the bus. Your little neighbourhood scores won't save you from a travelcard.'

Hannah laughed. 'A travelcard? When's the last time you took public transport, Guin?'

'Oh, I don't know, don't tease me. Oyster card or whatever it is now. I just use my phone these days. But I *do* prefer walking over taking the bus whenever I can help it.'

'We've still got to get you cycling!'

'In London? Absolutely not.' Guin shook her head at Martin.

'It's not as bad as the horror stories make out. My biggest concern is losing the damn thing. You wouldn't believe how the bike thieves operate these days. They're organised, they actually have gangs—'

'You didn't leave yours outside, did you?' John aimed a mean smile at Martin. 'I mean, I certainly wouldn't leave a bike like that around here.'

'Someone wouldn't let me bring it in. I'm not happy about that.'

He made a face at Hannah. There was still a slight charge between them, the electric current of former intimacy. Hannah looked away.

'Whatever, bring it inside if you really want to,' she said. 'Honestly, it's not as bad here as you're all making out. I actually like it. The area is vibrant and diverse and—'

'That's a whole lot of euphemisms for *bad* – no, no. Let me tell her. On our way here, we were hassled by a group of loitering youths.' John stretched out the 'oo' sound, puckering his lips. 'It shook Guin up a bit. Me too, to be honest. Who knows what they're capable of? Now, tell me this: why do we tolerate that sort of antisocial behaviour in our cities? Guin and I were listening to an excellent Derek Watson podcast on this issue just last week, actually – although these days it's virtually a thought crime to even mention Derek Watson.'

'Actually,' Hannah piped up, 'we profiled him last month. Didn't you see it?'

Internally she cringed. Why did she always say 'we' or 'my paper' or 'our readers' – in what conceivable way was it, were they, hers? She simply belonged to the *Tribune*'s regular pool of freelance writers, nothing more.

The Fifth Horseman, they'd headlined the profile presenting neo-New Atheism's newest 'new face'. Watson, a podcaster, commentator and now author, was given a double-page spread in the newspaper's culture insert. Presenting his gospel as secularist Buddhism and downplaying the recurrent Islamophobic threads throughout his work, most space was afforded to Watson's current passion: genetics research. 'If liberals want to follow the science on vaccines, we must also follow the science on race. Watson is leading the way,' concluded the piece, a resounding endorsement. Of course, the feature presented no actual 'science' on either count; the interviewer had failed GCSE biology, Hannah knew for a fact. Remembering this, a familiar injustice prickled at her cheeks. Why hadn't she been assigned that interview? Why was she still stuck profiling 'activists' instead of intellectuals? In the accompanying photographs (the *Tribune* had splashed out for a styled shoot), the podcaster appeared sophisticated and mildly academic, peering at the camera through square-rimmed glasses, dressed in a Loro Piana polo and slacks.

'Pffft.' John let out a low splutter. 'No doubt it was the usual sneering tone of the left-wing media. You're too far gone to tribalism to give Derek's ideas a fair airing. And that's all I'm asking for – a little time in the open marketplace of ideas. But you're too scared to agree to that, even. You know these ideas would win if you gave your readers a choice.'

Unsure of what to say, Hannah tilted her head to one side and frowned slightly.

'Our culture is degenerating,' John went on with an air of finality, 'anyone can see that. We need a robust media that's ready to take on the hard conversations if we want to slow this decline.'

'Have you heard of the, ah' – Martin paused and looked from Hannah to John – 'Universe 25?'

John shrugged. 'I can't say I'm familiar with it.'

'Is this the "rat utopia" you were telling me about?' Guin smiled across the table at Martin.

'Yes, that's it. Only it was mice rather than rats. A behavioural scientist called John Calhoun dreamt it up in the fifties. Essentially, Calhoun created a perfect mouse society, giving them shelter, warmth, food and water ad libitum. He built a specially designed structure: about three-by-three metres, with metal walls up to here.' He raised his arm high to illustrate. 'That was, I suppose, the only downside. The mice weren't allowed to leave.'

'Was it a utopia or a prison, then?' Guin laughed.

'Not a bad question.' Martin nodded. 'Calhoun called that "emigration prevention". He wanted his utopia to be a closed universe descended from just eight mice, all genetically perfect.'

'Go on, then.' Guin was game. 'How'd it all go awry?'

Martin smiled ominously. 'Death was absent. That is to say, Calhoun removed the *environmental* causes of death from his experimental universe. At first, all was well. The population thrived, growing exponentially until about a year in. You see, with the old mice neither dying nor leaving, younger ones couldn't find a place within the social system. The less dominant males withdrew, naturally. They were largely inactive, though prone to occasional bouts of violence.' He shrugged. 'Most females hid themselves away too, and the overall birth rate dropped. The remaining few mothers became aggressive, territorial. They abandoned, and sometimes even attacked, their young.'

Guin shook her head slightly.

'Mhm, Calhoun took a dim view of that behaviour too. He called this phenomenon the "behavioural sink", theorising that eliminating the causes of physical death led to a complete breakdown of society – a sort of spiritual death. Before long, the entire population succumbed.

'Obviously, there's a lot of parallels with our current sociopolitical, ah . . . moment,' Martin went on, in his slow and halting style. 'The strangest thing about it, I'd say, was how Calhoun wrote it up. The paper was published in a scientific journal, you understand. But he drew heavily on religious imagery, quoting liberally from the Bible. And he came up with these fantastical names for the different mice behaviours and groups. I suppose it was the right choice . . . He certainly captured the public's imagination.'

With his story apparently over, Martin leaned back once again and crossed his ankles.

'Well?' John's tone was incredulous. 'What's your point with all that?'

'Ah.' Martin tilted his head back and smiled at the sky. 'Perhaps increased religiosity in times such as these is a useful thing, a sort of human failsafe that can help us to recover . . . well, at least better than the mice did. One could draw that conclusion.'

Martin had, with some success, lightly embraced elements of the 'Judeo-Christian tradition' in his recent writing. He'd detected hints of it in the culture at large, and he wanted to be well positioned should the bourgeois position on religion shift. Culture writing was a delicate art; it necessitated a sensitivity to the social mood. He was part soothsayer, part analyst, part lyricist – and entirely willing to adopt whichever moral standpoint best helped him to fulfil those functions profitably.

'I don't think that's the right conclusion,' John said. 'At times like this we should reach for objectivity and rationality, not talking to the big spaghetti monster in the sky.'

'Ah, but' – Martin furrowed his brow – 'can we say, necessarily, that atheism is a more enlightened position? Arguably the practice of atheism is increasingly . . . dogmatic. What if atheism is just the newest mass religion?'

'A fair claim if you consider science dogma.' John spoke with strained equanimity. 'In which case, you probably are a religious nut.'

John's morosity tipped Martin's good humour over to

uncontrollable glee. He held his hands up as if to say 'Stop, no more' while his rumbling laughter subsided. Still wheezing, he offered John a conciliatory question: how was the world of science faring these days?

Grimacing as she sniffed at the small reservoir of wine in her large glass, Guin mimed exasperation. 'Don't get him started – please!'

But John launched into talk about his work with gusto.

'I don't know if you're aware' – a preamble, Hannah noticed, addressed to her alone – 'but I have just recently changed career.' He went on to explain that he had left the civil service for a healthtech analytics start-up. Did Hannah remember, John wondered, that his master's thesis had focused on the social ramifications of some cutting-edge genetic research called GWAS? He pronounced it first as 'gee-was', then spelled out the acronym. 'It turns out,' he went on without pausing for an answer, 'that, all these years later, GenetIQ is now actually applying this area of research. Isn't that exciting? I couldn't quite believe it myself, but I knew I had to get involved.' As soon as their research grant went through, John approached the company discreetly. 'And, well, one thing led to another, you could say.' He smirked at Hannah. 'It's crazy, you know. What we can do with data these days. We're starting with recruitment companies for now, but the long-term goal is to roll this out in broader areas of society – like social housing, policing, education, and of course the NHS.'

'But what exactly *is* it?' Hannah interjected.

'Basically,' said John, relishing the opportunity to give his explanation, 'it's what we call "meatspace alignment". As I'm sure you know, lots of researchers are doing excellent work on AI alignment, making sure the inevitable AGI is lined up with the best interests of us humans. But we have to stand up to our side of the bargain too. We need to understand who's best suited to what, and guide the right humans to the right roles.

'That's where GenetIQ comes in. We use DNA samples to predict the likelihood of various life outcomes. Positive and negative. And some are *really* positive, like there's a few people we should literally bribe to become sperm donors, their DNA is that good!'

John tried to keep his tone spontaneous and light. Guin smiled, without meeting his eyes. She was disappointed, John knew. Right up until he actually left the civil service, she'd maintained a hope that he would eventually manoeuvre his uninspiring career beginning into a meaningful position in the political machine. But it wasn't that simple. In government, he simply could not distinguish himself from the herd. Excluded from the choicest placements after completing the Fast Track, he had slotted in at Research Funding Support, where he spent his days writing reports about inane grant applications, so that some other cog in the machine could read his reports and decide whether or not taxpayers would foot the bill. Career progression was painfully slow. Working harder did not yield any noticeable benefit. Those markers for success, the easy public-schoolboy charm, a leisurely, assured manner when speaking of geopolitics, were unconvincing on him. He was relegated to the multitude: the lower middle and working classes, plus the smattering of minorities, that made up the bulk of the grunt-level workforce.

But how to explain it to Guin? She was of that other type, the quiet-word type, the personal-recommendations-and-un-advertised-jobs type. Her approach was no use to someone like him. There was nothing for it: he'd had to follow his gut. He had spent so many years frustrated and, yes, emasculated. Guin wasn't blameless in this either: to his dismay she had refused his last name, citing feminism, though he suspected *Le Mesurier* suited her better than his pedestrian Gibbs. All the more reason, he'd told himself, to strike out on his own path. Without a family name to depend on, he would bet instead on genetics.

'But how' – Hannah's voice had the timbre of a whine – 'how could DNA tell you whether a person can do a job? DNA doesn't tell you anything about education or experience or—'

'It's always about the "lived experience" with *your* tribe, isn't it?' John shook his head.

'That's not what I mean at all! I'm saying that one candidate might have years of relevant experience in a similar job, but you wouldn't know it from just a strand of their hair.'

'Okay, well, that's a fair enough point. And you'll be glad to hear that no one is proposing throwing away CVs.

Our analysis empowers clients to *supplement* a candidate's CV with additional data about potential traits and likely outcomes. More relevant information, not less. It's nothing sinister, there's no reason to scream and shout about it.'

'What kind of traits do you measure?' Martin asked.

'Well, IQ is the big one, as our name suggests. Our predictive acc—'

'Oh, come on,' Hannah protested. 'Everyone knows IQ is classist, and racist!'

'Racist?' John laughed bitterly. 'How on earth could a simple logic and reasoning test be *racist*? Unless you think acknowledging the possibility of diversity in intelligence is racist. At the end of the day it's just data. Data isn't good or bad, it has no agenda – it's just a way of measuring our world objectively.'

'But environment must have something to do with it,' Hannah said miserably.

'A very reasonable point' – John had thoroughly warmed to his theme – 'and don't worry, our model takes that into account, using a mathematical formula known as the *heritability equation*.'

As a student, he'd struggled with maths and avoided all but the mandatory statistics courses during his sociology degree. Now, he treasured the subject's unassailable authority, particularly among the numerically illiterate. Frame any claim as an equation, he found, and you could consider the thing as good as proved. Still, John wished that he had a background in the hard sciences. There was a clear hierarchy at GenetIQ, with statisticians, biologists and data scientists at the top end. His own place was further down the food chain. Instead of reading grant applications, he now wrote them. It wasn't a material difference to his previous life, but he was excited to play a role in the future, however small. His efforts helped to feed the mysterious 'model', that enormous, greedy algorithm that gobbled up every datum it was fed. Human biodiversity had fascinated him from the moment he'd encountered the concept, whispered about in online forums and university mailing lists. Immediately, he appreciated the implications of this kind of genetics research. He believed in the science, even if he couldn't fully grok it. It would be ludicrous to expect every individual to understand the nuances of every technological advance of modern life. Statistics and science required a degree of faith. He'd made his peace with this.

'You'll be pleased to know that our research often benefits people from a less advantageous socio-economic background.' He smiled patronisingly. 'Sometimes the data shows potential that isn't present in exam results, for instance.'

'I see,' Hannah said. Then, after a pause: 'I don't know. It does seem like a risky line of enquiry.'

Little wonder, John mused, that the public had such a mean understanding of the topic. When idiots like Hannah were the conduit to the everyday man, the ignorant were leading the stupid. Of course reactionary outrage was preferable to admitting ignorance. He was glad he'd found other, better, sources of information. The books, blogs and podcasts that would follow the science wherever it led, even if – fuck it, especially if – the end result wasn't woke. A fear of facts was holding the country back. He looked into Hannah's dull, unthinking face; the inadvertent herald of Western society's decline, stupidly chewing an olive.

'A slippery slope down to eugenics, eh?' said Martin, irreverent as ever.

'No, no, I won't accept that. This is *science* – and what you're doing there is suppressing it. I don't care if you're joking. These ideas, this research, this science is being silenced. It has huge ramifications for how we should run our society and yet where is it in your magazines, your newspapers? You guys refuse to engage with it. Look.' John paused, modulating his voice. 'I understand that measuring genetic group differences has a . . . complicated history. And I know that it can be an uncomfortable topic – even among friends. But suppressing the research isn't the answer. If we did that, we'd still believe that the sun rotates around the earth. For the sake of our future society, we need to face the facts.'

'Oh, stop pretending it's all so deep,' Guin sighed. 'You read a Harry Potter fan fiction when you were a student and it derailed your entire life. It's possible to appreciate statistics without making it your whole identity.' She turned to Martin and Hannah. 'Did you know, I had to talk him out of getting a Bayes' theorem *tattoo*.'

'In the time of *Love Island* and identity politics, I'd say that appreciating the scientific method is a valid point of differentiation,' John said with dignity.

'I think you're too down on *Love Island*, actually. Martin and I watched a few episodes last season and you know what? I liked it. It captures something of modern Britain, I think. It's who we are as a nation.'

Hannah scoffed. Then, as if surprised by her own reaction, explained herself quickly: 'You don't mean that, right? It comes off as snobbery . . .'

'Well, it's not. Not at all.' Guin's features sharpened in the falling light.

'I don't approve of it,' said John. 'We're sleepwalking into *Idiocracy* – you shouldn't be cheering it on, Guin. Not even ironically.'

'Well, now.' Martin drew himself up. 'I'll admit I've written about it once or twice. I don't think it's as bad as all that. I think it creates a sense of community across the nation. It harks back to a time when we all used to tune in to one of five channels and watch the same thing. Before cable TV and the internet fractured everyone's media diet into individually tuned bubbles. That's a good thing, in my book. Just the kind of unity we need as a country.'

'It's the last fucking thing this country needs.'

In the abrupt silence, John picked up his wine glass. His thin lips pressed tight together as his eyes stared out cold and defiant. For a moment, no one spoke. Tucking his jaw in towards his neck, he half-shrugged. Without sipping, he returned the glass to the table with painstaking tremolo intensity. A car roared faintly, as if from a great distance. A deep, oceanic whoosh of acceleration. Cloistered within the garden's wooden fences, their quartet sat still.

'I hear you,' Hannah said at last, pressing into the quiet. Indeed, John's concerns were largely the concerns of her editors, effectively making them her concerns too, and the unstated theses of the pieces she and her colleagues all pitched and wrote. An entire ecosystem was convulsing and straining to validate John's worldview. Guin rubbed his forearm absently. Hannah watched the soft ovals her hand traced, the little pink-glazed nails.

It hadn't been like this when they were students. On countless evenings, the four of them had sat around talking late into the night. Guin squinting and playing with long strands of her hair as she listened to whatever new cause Hannah was either supporting or vehemently opposed to. Not prone to the boys' bravado or Hannah's earnest energy, she'd always remained quietly aloof. John, too, had mostly kept a cool head. Of course they debated hot subjects, but John's opinions had felt ironically held back then. Such vigorous arguments were just sport. If anything, Hannah had been more emotionally invested than him, feeling attacked whenever her beliefs were mocked or dismissed. Unable to treat her own identity as a purely theoretical concept, their rhetorical jabs often felt personal. But Guin, Martin and John had existed comfortably beyond the reach of words. Untouchable, until now. Hannah wondered what had caused this change, and whether she could make an article of it.

'Right, of course. You *hear* me,' John sneered. Tilting his chin towards Guin, he muttered through clenched teeth. 'I told you. Coming here was a complete waste of—'

'O-kay!' Martin clapped his palms together. 'Come on, Hannah, let's go rescue my bike. If it's not too late.'

Hannah allowed herself to be bustled back along inside. The kitchen's humid, buttery air had turned sour. Martin retraced his earlier path through the flat in a few brisk strides. After fumbling with the latch, he stepped out and surveyed the cramped front yard.

'Ah, there's my girl.' His glibness masked real relief. 'Still out here.'

'That was crazy-intense,' Hannah said from the doorway. She shivered and folded her arms across her chest. 'What on earth's going on with John?'

'Never mind him.' Martin waved a breezy hand. 'Too much time on the intellectual dark web.'

Leaning against the low front wall, he fixed his eyes on Hannah and watched as blotches of red spread across her face and neck. He searched for any hint of change in her soft, familiar form. Her byline in *Alazon* had flummoxed him. Granted, the piece wasn't going to win a Pulitzer. It lacked direction and could have used a sharper edit to tone down the melodrama and moralising. Still, the writing demonstrated a certain savvy; it had been provocative enough to amuse Twitter for a fortnight, and had spawned plenty of think-pieces offline too. The unimaginative, easily flustered girl he'd known wasn't up to such a feat. Hannah's pale legs were goosebumped beyond the too-short hem of her skirt. She had pretty decent legs, and always did enjoy showing them off . . . Martin had appreciated that about her, at one time. But really, who was wearing miniskirts these days? That was the problem with Hannah, and the thing he couldn't reconcile in all this. She was culturally clueless, practically allergic to the zeitgeist. How had she pulled it off?

'I'll be honest, I had an ulterior motive here tonight.' His words were slow and deliberate. 'I wanted to see you – I need to ask you something.'

'Anything.' Hannah's answer was immediate, expected. Martin smiled.

'Lenny,' he said at last. 'What's the deal with her?'

The question flopped between them.

'Lenny,' Hannah repeated eventually. 'What's Lenny got to do with us?'

'Well . . .' Martin drew the discourse particle out in a long exhale. 'You know her. And I'm interviewing her at Cartmel.'

'Cartmel?'

It wasn't a question, not really. But Martin leapt into a response. He blathered on about how important Cartmel was. Arguably the most influential cultural event in the UK. It moved the national conversation. Politicians and CEOs were often in attendance. A good showing at Cartmel would unleash unimaginable new opportunities for him – indeed, he'd spent considerable time imagining just what those opportunities might entail. This was it, Hannah realised, what the evening was really about. Information. She couldn't make out what Martin was saying. The facts of the situation were swirling and rearranging themselves, her hopes twisting into knots of disappointment.

She knew Martin, or, at least, knew who he used to be. The idealistic young writer who kept a battered, signed copy of *The War Against Cliché* in the bottom of his rucksack, then satchel, then pannier. She remembered that. These days, he took any excuse to lay into his namesake, in what was no doubt the literary expression of an Oedipus impulse. He was a Serious Critic now. So often paywalled, his words carried more weight than hers. Sprawling, multi-thousand-word book reviews bearing his byline were published in prestigious literary journals. Getty Images had a tag for him. He was a staff critic at *Perspective!* magazine. He'd managed to ingratiate himself with an elite crowd by understanding how to exploit people and when to throw them away. Tonight, however briefly, Hannah was exploitable again.

Well, more fool Martin. Her consolation was bittersweet. Whatever special insight into Lenny he'd hoped for, Hannah wouldn't be able to provide it. Even if she wanted to. She hadn't heard from Lenny in months.

That email, Lenny's proposal, had been a lifeline. Hannah

had thrown herself into the story, tracking down Lenny's list of interviewees and making meticulous notes and recordings. Under Lenny's attentive tutelage, Hannah had bent and arranged paltry facts into a compelling narrative, sculpting vivid characters from the putty of everyday people. Together, they'd transformed real life into something else: bigger, brighter, more engaging. Yet somehow, after all that, despite the undeniable *bond* between the pair, Lenny had ghosted Hannah. Right after arranging the article's publication. Calls, emails, WhatsApps – all went unanswered. Hannah was paid nearly £4,000 for the piece, a life-saving amount. The article's virality raised her profile; she was booked on podcasts and gained a few hundred new followers, tipping her over into four digits. Exciting, while it lasted. Until the story moved on without her and other journalists swooped in, publishing updates and new takes without even mentioning Hannah's name. She tried to move on herself, sending out dozens of fresh pitches. But the entire process was chicken-and-egg. No one would talk to her until she had a publication committed, and no publication seemed willing to accept a pitch without background. Soon enough, she found herself scrapping around for the same old freelance work: five-hundred-word summaries of the latest multicultural dreck passing for contemporary women's fiction. The adaptation deal had brought in more money, enough for a deposit. Enough money to change everything and nothing, it turned out. She still couldn't penetrate Martin's world.

'Sorry,' she said quietly. 'Lenny and I haven't . . . touched base in a while. I can't help you.'

'"Help" is overstating it a bit. I don't need— I mean, I'm not expecting her to be a particularly challenging interviewee. Quite the opposite. Still, it's Cartmel. It's a huge deal. So if you can share any little insights into Lenny beforehand, well' – he stepped towards her, a half-smile animating his face – 'I'd be very grateful.'

'No' was a difficult word. Particularly because Hannah had always said yes to Martin. There were other words she could say, things she had longed for the chance to say. But now, now that she finally held Martin's attention again? Those words failed her. She couldn't compress all the years of hurt, resentment and affection into ordinary sentences. Anything she said would sound hackneyed, inviting his cutting scorn. Instead, Hannah gave him what he wanted, the little she knew. She offered up everything she could remember about Lenny's theories and worldview. Much too quickly, she exhausted her knowledge. Pausing, she tried to think of something more to say.

'Ah, yes.' Martin nodded. 'Class is the new race. Economic inequality is the most pernicious social ill, and so on. We've taken that line at *Perspective!* too. Yes.' Retreating into his own thoughts, Martin seemed to forget Hannah entirely. He mumbled quietly, stared at his shoes. Finally, he looked up and squeezed her shoulder.

'Thanks, Han,' he said.

The platitude was delivered quickly, but kindly. Martin turned back to his bike and detached the lock from the metal gate. It was over. Hannah's usefulness to him, her moment, had elapsed. She stood aside, letting him carry the ludicrous contraption indoors. She watched the back wheel smudge against the wall as he negotiated the narrow corridor.

This was a strange phase of life: an age when waists thickened, hair thinned and skin lost elasticity. Hannah had seen it in her own reflection, in the tired lines that traced the crevices of her face. John was different too. He appeared faded now, his hair curling in soft wisps rather than thick tufts; the contours of his jaw too visible beneath the lean flesh of his cheeks. Guin, of course, had fared better. She still glowed with good living and expensive products, all those little bottles and jars in the department store. Martin alone had actually benefited from the passage of time. His facial features were sharper, his body hardened and muscular, since he'd discovered biking as a means of both recreation and transport. His shabby clothes now seemed deliberately neglected, signalling a mind focused on more intellectual pursuits than fashion. She looked down at her own hands, hanging limp against her thighs.

Martin had used her.

Lenny had used her.

The truth clicked into awful clarity. Everything Lenny had said about choosing Hannah – the talk of potential and promise and working-class solidarity – it meant nothing. Hannah had grown up a few towns over from Queensbury; near enough, and Lenny had been insistent on this point, to tell the story with *authenticity*. She'd demanded a specific kind of idealised Englishness: that of the unspoilt village, not Bradford's muddy melting pot. And, like a complete idiot, Hannah had obliged. Making up rubbish about knowing the Aldertons – even milking cows, for fuck's sake. She'd lied about her own life, becoming a stupid caricature, a convenient identity for Lenny's article. Because it was Lenny's article, wasn't it? Despite Hannah's name above the words. The story had catapulted Lenny to stardom. Hannah had been left behind.

All around her, the neighbouring houses glared, transformed by dark shadows into strange faces. How long had she stood there? It could have been minutes or hours. A cool breeze slapped at her, but Hannah hardly noticed. Perhaps truth could inoculate her from physical pain. The chicken was probably overdone. She should see to it. Blinking, breathing, turning. Hannah stepped back inside.

WEYBRIDGE

'Why don't you hate me?'

'I'm busy, not everything is about you.'

'But surely this is about me. Claire. Look at me. Please, Claire.'

Richard watched as his wife, after all she was still his wife, stopped wiping the counter and turned to face him.

'What's gotten into you?' she said.

'I – I don't know. I feel I've treated you badly.'

'You have.'

Wounded by this frankness, Richard gawped at her. He'd expected – oh, what? She had every right to despise him.

'What do you want from me, Richard? We're here, we're getting along. I don't know why you're dredging all this up again.'

Richard's face crumpled; he coughed, craning away from her as he tried to choke the emotion back down. He'd never cried like this before, standing up in a brightly lit kitchen. He couldn't bear it. Shoulders shuddering, he squeezed his eyes shut, willing it away. Then, her arms around him; the soapy clinical stinging in his nostrils from the cloth she still held. Pressing his face to her neck, he breathed in: earthy skin, unwashed hair and Laundress-spritzed wool. The scent of Claire the mother, mothering him now as he swallowed his sobs.

'Come on,' she said, or whispered. 'Come on.'

He sat on a barstool as Claire corralled Rosie for bed. The small child, who still had the absurd proportions of a toddler, was surprisingly articulate. She was not ready, she insisted, for bed. In a shrill and certain voice, she listed the things she'd rather do first. After naming five or six, she looked around the room for further ideas. Her eyes fixed on Richard, shining and unsteady, then continued past him to the dining area.

'Folding *serviettes*!' she shrieked, delighted at her novel idea.

Recognising himself as superfluous to the bedtime routine, to his wife, her daughter, and their lives, he waved a wordless goodbye and left. He tried to close the front door gently behind him, but it was stuck. Yanking, hard, on the brass knob, he managed to force it shut. The resounding thud shamed him. Why wasn't he around to fix this for his family? Because of him, his daughter would grow up in a house with stiff, awkward doors.

He could let himself back in and mend it, possibly even spend the night in a guest room . . . Could they slip into a new, familial pattern? Claire might have him back, despite his publicised betrayals and her evident self-sufficiency. She was the type, he knew instinctively, to sacrifice her own happiness in favour of a veneer of normality for Rosie.

No, not just yet. He'd been offered a few soft landings – old colleagues and friends had, after his initial period of total radioactivity, reached out. In due course he would likely take one of these up, attempt to rebuild things. The story's publication had been a *career-limiting* event, but he'd find a comfortable sinecure. It wasn't the future he'd imagined for himself, but then, when did life ever bend to expectation? For tonight, he was content to wallow in the strangeness of his present circumstances, the fibrous edges of his old, torn-apart life. 'Like wet tissue paper' – where had that phrase come from? He grimaced, taken at once back to those awful NCT classes, and that grotesquely talkative woman who googled too much and blabbed even more . . . 'Do you know what it means for a perineum to tear?' she'd whispered to him before popping a custard cream into her little mouth. Then she'd uttered those words, flashing him with half-chewed biscuit – smugly certain that the image would take horrifying hold in his mind. Of everyone on their Kensington course, held in a windowless back room that usually hosted zero-gravity yoga, the woman had chosen Richard as her confidant. She'd spotted that he wasn't quite like the others.

'I can't stand her,' he told Claire after the class, steadying her arm as she took off her shoes and then dropped, exhausted, onto the sofa.

'She's alright,' Claire sighed. 'Just scared, and alone. I'm not sure I could hack it, going into that room week after week without you. You're really good in there, really supportive. That's probably why she's so keen on you.'

Claire's body had changed in the obvious ways, but he'd noticed subtle differences too. He couldn't find words to describe it; in photos from before, she seemed under-formed in comparison. Claire swivelled her feet up to the seat and eased herself onto her back.

'Well,' he said, 'I'd better catch up on email.' Claire's eyes fluttered shut and she nodded, then laid her head on the armrest. He took her left hand and kissed the backs of her fingers.

Those months whizzed past at fast-forward speed: finding the house in Surrey, packing up their lives and moving in. Welcoming the baby. Four bleary weeks of paternal leave. Back in the office, exhausted, he couldn't quite convince himself that it was all real. That picturesque home life. Perhaps it wasn't; he never could adjust his self-image to that of a 'parent'. Whenever he interacted with the baby, he felt fraudulent. Baffled by its inscrutable cries. The deepening bond of understanding between mother and child only excluded him further. Better to spend his nights in the city, he finally decided, than to come home late and intrude on their intimate domesticity. He took Claire's lack of complaint as unspoken relief.

Turning away from the front door now, he drew in a sweeping breath. The evening was mild; he could walk to the station. Fluttering boughs of yellow-green leaves waved encouragement. He almost never experienced this time of day outside. Most of his evenings, like his mornings, had been spent breathing artificially cooled air in artificially brightened rooms. To notice the appeal of a balmy evening – that was progress, he told himself. This new-found calm, despite his persistent bouts of inexplicable crying, marked a step forward.

At first, he'd felt violated. What he'd believed was a shared understanding, even trust, between him and that girl Hannah, had proved to be a cruel confidence trick. He couldn't quite, not at first, hold the entirety of it in his mind, or see its full form – he was still up too close, still groping his way around a single edge of the violation. Despite this lack of perspective, he knew, or was beginning to understand, the magnitude of his fuck-up. The grossness of her caricature, and its orthogonality to the truth of him, was stunning; he remained stunned as the perverse parody took hold within the British media.

He had tried, at the beginning, to counter the inaccuracies, naively believing that his tormentors had an interest in *facts*. A self-identified 'fact-checker for the magazine' had emailed him to query his date of birth and surname shortly before the piece went online. Once he'd recovered enough fortitude, Richard had sent a new email to this fact-checker listing every issue with the piece: beginning with the claim that he owned a 'solid gold bar' and ending with Hannah's misuse of 'begging the question'. No reply. Meanwhile, the inaccuracies – or, to call them what they really were, the lies – spread rapidly, amplifying with each repetition.

Eventually his efforts brought him to a cramped office, squeezed into the top floor of a building on a higgledy-piggledy back street near Oxford Circus. Hannah and her agent, Marie, had agreed to meet and discuss what Marie delicately termed his 'concerns'. It was the first time he'd seen Hannah since their last interview, when she'd hugged him and told him to take care. She looked well. After the adaptation rights had sold, she'd bought a house. He knew this because she wrote a personal essay on how home ownership had changed her taste in music, or painting, or something equally ridiculous. As far as he could tell, the authorial tone was not ironic. Had she ever truly opposed capitalism, or merely her own disenfranchisement? Not that the distinction mattered, he supposed, as long as the grievance could be monetised.

Home ownership hadn't changed her views on him, in any case. A contemptuous smirk greeted him before she did. Presumably because his money didn't come from appropriating other people's lives. Or, possibly, because people like her couldn't secure art-preference-changing mortgages without people like him, who provided statistical confidence that the debt wasn't totally worthless. He knew that smirk; it was the same smirk he'd seen directed at his father, and at all the grubby people who constructed houses – whether out of bricks and mortar or through securitisation.

He looked again at Hannah. Clearly some man had shoved his hand up her skirt – or, worse, *hadn't* – and now she was taking it out on him, ruining his life. That was an ugly thought, the sort of thought her pathetic caricature might think. He regretted it. But also, after reading such a distortion of himself, how could he not think it? How could he ever exist as a person, separate from that article, again?

'You said you wanted to get to the truth,' he began after the terse pleasantries, letting indignation swell within his chest. 'But half of what you wrote was just made up. It's libellous.'

'"The truth" is ambiguous' – Marie swooped in before Hannah could speak. 'It's not absolute. Hannah's journalism was a composition of multiple accounts, or "truths", creating a complex picture for her readers to interpret. Her journalism is no less true, no less honest, for its plurality. In fact I think it's more honest. More of a reflection of how the world really is – outside of your privileged bubble.'

'Privileged?' He shook his head at that. 'Not everything is a culture war. Some things just *are*, and others aren't. Some things were, some weren't. We must be able to agree on that much, at least.'

Tilting her head to the left, Marie absently whispered something to Hannah, who nodded and stood up reluctantly, avoiding the hazardous piles of books and papers as she charted a path out of the small room.

'Look,' Marie said, once Hannah had closed the door. 'I've listened to some of the recordings. You don't come off well. I don't think "releasing the tapes" here, or whatever your retribution fantasy is, will go in your favour. You're hardly a sympathetic character.' With a slight nod, Marie pointed through the door's window to Hannah, who was at that moment struggling with a coffee machine. 'Besides this adaptation deal, she's got nothing. But, despite all the self-pity, you've still got lots to lose. *Alazon* magazine's parent company is a major news organisation. If you bring a libel case against them, they'll completely exhaust your financial resources and destroy whatever's left of your reputation. They will drag you through the mud. In the end, you and Hannah will both wind up with nothing, though she can always write a contrite personal essay and get back to her old life. She'll be fine. What will you do then, exactly?'

He could think of nothing to say. Without his corporate exoskeleton he found himself appallingly vulnerable, and more avoidant of conflict than ever. He barely managed to keep from crying as he sat there. He sniffed, shrugged. It was hopeless. Swathed in scarves and shawls, with silvery hair cut to just above her shoulders, Marie looked like she had the capacity for kindness. She used it then, sweetening her voice to a conciliatory coo.

'I tell you what. Give it another month or two, and this'll blow over. Really. If the show goes ahead, and that's a big if, they'll use a different name for your character anyway. Something less . . . well, you know. None of this is about you *personally*, it's just a good story. Bread-and-circus stuff. A shiny new diversion will come along soon enough. Here's what I think, Richard. Not that you asked, but I'll tell you all the same. Here's what you do next: go home to your wife and daughter. Wait this out.'

She let out a tinkling little laugh.

'Oh,' she said on Hannah's re-entry, raising an amused brow at the precariously balanced trio of coffee mugs. 'I don't think we'll need those after all, will we, Richard? We're just about done.'

He took Marie's counsel, more or less, and resigned himself to the onslaught. The press bashed him with a gleeful ferocity. And it extended beyond him – Rachel, whom he'd never meant to drag into any of this, was discovered and hounded. She was 'papped'. Snaps of her leaving Itsu with two boxes of sushi; striding into Barry's, gym bag under arm, hair piled up in a messy bun; her corporate headshot, even – were published alongside a lone landscape photograph of Claire and Rosie outside the family home, staring glumly into the camera. A passing description as an 'enterprising intern' in a *Guardian* opinion piece was the final straw. That had hurt her deeply, Richard knew. As a professional – highly qualified and successful in her own right – facing sneering innuendo in the newspaper she often read was far more degrading than being labelled 'SOS: SAUCY office SIDEPIECE' in the tabloids. Understandably, Rachel gave up, transferring to the NY office and telling Richard to lose her fucking number.

Claire was spared. Through a family connection, her parents arranged a sympathetic profile of her, and that dignified, solemn portrait was allowed to stand unchallenged and untarnished. The papers seemed satisfied to rally around this ill-treated wife, taking up her cause, even if she'd have much preferred it to be let well alone. Eventually the interest waned, though a long tail of attention persisted further than either of them had expected. Richard was too appealing to ignore, too easy to criticise and moralise about.

'Don't you want to set things straight?' 'No one's heard your side of things.' 'After all this time, we still have no idea of who you really are.' 'Who is Richard Spencer? That's what I want to know. I want to hear from *you*, Richard. I'm on your side.' In the flurry of daily emails, WhatsApps and voicemails, one persistently understanding voice wormed its way in. After weeks of deliberation, Richard agreed to talk. A profile would run in men's magazine *HQ* and – the voice promised – set the record straight.

The journalist who turned up was a spry, energetic man. He hobbled into Richard's apartment, encumbered by a large boot on his left leg.

'Mishap on the slopes!' He smiled broadly, then asked where Richard usually skied.

Richard didn't ski. He'd never learned to, and by the time he realised how important a skill it was, it was too late. He felt embarrassed seeing men his age – back at that time, twenty-four seemed like a ripe old age – fretfully launching themselves down treacherous white mountains in the hope that their career prospects would improve. Reluctantly, he'd joined a few trips with Claire's friends, but had always restricted himself to the après-ski bar, sipping beers glumly as he stared out at the vast, frozen landscapes.

Holidays were supposed to be hot! As kids, he and his brother Nick had spent two weeks every summer at a caravan park in Devon, scrabbling over rocky beaches and gulping down sour scrumpy with their fish-and-chips dinners. Gazing into the sea, Richard could sit for hours in the saline breeze, tossing an occasional cold chip to the gulls and watching them scrap. The one year his family booked a package holiday to Mallorca, the boys had reigned like princes, seduced by the stretches of yellow sand, the dependably hot sunshine and the unlimited servings at the buffet-style meals. Could that childish version of him ever have imagined the disconcerting blue solidity of a cloudless sky in Courchevel? How the bleak expanse of expensive *nothingness* spread out impossibly far in all directions? It was a different universe.

'Really? You're missing out!' said the little journalist cheerfully.

Richard Spencer prefers luxury private beach resorts to skiing in the Alps.

'Now then.' He clapped his hands together. 'Shall we begin with all the bother about this golden bar?'

That it wasn't a real gold bar, merely gold-plated tungsten, had been perhaps the most frustrating inaccuracy. Richard was keen to address this; the image of himself with enough spare cash that he'd waste it so spectacularly appalled him. The bar was *decorative* – that's why he hadn't minded leaving it at the farm. It wasn't a sophisticated counterfeit, but an obvious fake! A tacky indulgence that, for whatever reason, had appealed to him. He was guilty of a lot of things, but this was evidence only of his crass new-money tastes, not extreme wealth. Pieces of designer furniture, the kinds often featured in *HQ*, as a matter of fact, were typically more expensive than that 'gold bar'.

'You think that gold bar's expensive? The chair you're sitting on cost more,' boasts an unrepentant Spencer.

'That's still a great deal of money . . .' the journalist said, sounding less like the friendly voice on the phone and more like the self-assured snobbery of the chattering classes. 'How can you justify your level of wealth at a time when so many people are struggling – wouldn't you say it's immoral to be a billionaire?'

What did people think a billionaire was? Did they seriously believe Richard might open up his payslip and find *One billion pounds sterling* written at the bottom? Altogether, his assets were worth a few million, that much was true. Most middle-class families, if they took a serious look at everything they owned – including pensions, including homes – would find themselves to be paper millionaires too. Certainly, this journalist himself was one. How did it become so contentious to point that out?

Spencer is so out of touch that he believes, quite sincerely, that almost everyone is a millionaire . . . and that being a billionaire is no big deal!

'Well, let's put that aside, then. Don't you feel your specific way of making money is a bit unethical? You're not helping society very much as a banker, are you?'

Richard couldn't quite understand what it was about him that rankled these people so much. Hadn't he simply done what he was supposed to do? He'd taken the eleven-plus, made it into the grammar school, and simply followed that life path to its inevitable conclusion. He didn't hurt anyone, he didn't exploit anyone. He tried, as much as was possible, to work hard and fair. After the crash, he'd moved into regulatory risk . . . working to prevent another crisis. And, as the divisional head, he'd ensured that there were women in senior roles, along with a broadly diverse management team. Indeed, he now had a network of colleagues who credited him as a friend and a mentor. He was proud of that legacy. His was not the monoculture of commoditised socialism, with its vague, moralistic promise to end discrimination. He was actually doing his part by hiring qualified candidates and giving them the same chance at success that he himself had received. All these 'writers' did, as far as Richard could tell, was spread gossip for fun and profit, stoking outrage and discontent without actually fixing anything.

One thing becomes clear, as he waxes lyrical about the virtues of investment banks: Spencer truly believes that 'greed is good'. At times, he seems to physically hold himself back from proclaiming it.

'We bailed you out,' said the little journalist, indignant. 'Privatised gains, public losses! How can you defend your role in the credit crunch?'

What did this man know of the credit crunch? Nothing – no doubt he'd been totally insulated from it. Richard had lived it, he'd fought his way through it and survived. Still a young VP at the time, he'd run a small prop trading desk, with a grad and two associates working for him. He took each in turn to a spare office and stumbled through the words. The contents of their desks, he promised, would be packed up and mailed to their homes. Was that true? Richard wasn't sure. The people who packed desks up into shipping boxes, those who arranged delivery and printed off labels, and the others who carted the boxes down to the mailroom and signed the collection slips – did those people still have their jobs? One by one, he escorted each of his now former employees down to the building entrance, with its newly militarised atmosphere enforced by extra security guards. He asked for their access cards and left them, standing bewildered in the bright daylight.

After the third trip down, he walked back into the lift alone and felt his stomach sink as the floors ticked up. Stepping out, he walked over to the glass doors and tapped himself in. The sudden blue-grey emptiness of it struck him; the floor looked like a drained ocean. For the first time, he noticed the little abstract repeating patterns across the faded carpet tiles. The televisions all played the same disastrous news loop. A few people were gathered beneath one, with the sound on low, watching with a bloodless quiet he hadn't seen since the Tube bombings. He tried to cling to that perspective, however tasteless the comparison: no one was dying.

'Spence?'

On hearing the call, he trudged obediently to his boss's office, ready to take one final trip down in the elevator. But the news was good, so far as anything could be considered good that day. He would be kept on, at least for the foreseeable, to close out the positions of his desk, along with a few others'. Then, possibly, they could use him on the market-making side. Not the sort of work he thought he'd be doing at this point in his life. But he was grateful for it. Especially when, a few weeks later, his boss's own avatar went grey in the system.

Whatever it took, Richard had to hang on. Make himself indispensable. Much as his brother hated London, Nick had driven down one evening to talk. Over a beer, Richard listened to how bad things had got. His father's company was being squeezed – still on the hook for suppliers' bills, while customers ignored invoices and reneged on contracts. Middle-class men like that journalist, deciding to cancel their loft conversions and double extensions, without a thought about who would shoulder the cost. Already weakened by the death of their mother a few years earlier, their dad had frozen up completely. He couldn't find a way through it. Nick fiddled with a damp napkin, avoiding eye contact with Richard, while he apologised for asking for help in this way. Their father was a man who'd worked hard and honestly, every day of his adult life, and so far that approach had paid off. Now, the business that he'd hoped to pass on to Nick was on the brink of insolvency.

There was no question, of course. They were brothers, family. Of course, of course, Richard repeated like a prayer. They clung to one another tightly at the end of the night. As if they'd been lost for decades. And so Rich made himself *indispensable*, taking on any task and staying late every night – on hand to answer anything, fix anything, do anything to keep his family afloat.

Expecting Claire to understand wasn't fair; how could she know the pressure that he was under? She tried to be supportive, and patient, but she was increasingly exasperated with her tired, distracted husband.

'You're never home for dinner,' she said one evening, her bottom lip turned out in a sulk. Their dining table was elaborately set, complete with two plates of (presumably) cold food. Claire gestured towards this tableau; she had a mischievous, dramatic streak, especially when angry. 'And that's made *me* into the sort of wife who complains that her husband's not home for dinner.'

What could Rich say to that? He apologised and promised he'd make more of an effort. Even as he spoke, they both knew it wasn't true. He couldn't risk his position. His family, the one that he was born into, was thoroughly dependent on him.

'I don't know why we can't just ask Daddy.' Her use of 'Daddy' in such situations, once whimsical and endearing, now grated on him. Claire's parents liked shopping for bargains at Lidl and Aldi, but their daughter slumming it with the son of an Essex brickie . . . that was going a bit far. Asking for money would vindicate their worst beliefs about him.

'I can't ask your dad,' he sighed, 'to help out *my* dad. No man wants to be put into that kind of a position.'

'I see.' Claire watched him as he drank a Peroni straight from the bottle. Her cold eyes told him that she did in fact see everything about him, and had come away distinctly unimpressed. 'You won't ask for help because of your own chauvinistic hang-ups. I suppose it's better that we're miserable than you upset the patriarchy.'

'That's not – not what I meant. I just . . .'

There was nothing he could say. Claire had never understood that to her parents he was the worst thing that had ever happened to her. And to his family, 'money' wasn't a guaranteed quantity, flowing like water from the taps. This was a strain he bore alone in their relationship.

'Claire. I'm sorry but I've been at it since five a.m. this morning. Do you think we could talk about this another time. Please?'

Then she cried. And he apologised, and comforted her, and they talked, reminding themselves of what it was they'd liked about each other in the first place. When he crept out of bed in the dark hours of the next morning, she bid him goodbye with soft, earnest kisses. Still, those little resentments were impossible to plaster over. It was during that time, Richard could see now, that they had come apart. Before the house, Rosie, everything else. Claire's parents had been right, after all.

It was getting chilly; he'd been rooted to the doorstep for nearly an hour. The thought of leaving, walking away from his family again, gave him a sense of unease. He had not, could not, shake off the destructive fear that some vague, bad thing was still on its way. This same nagging, inexplicable fear had driven him to buy the farm, along with the small-denomination gold bars. Even before that he'd bought freeze-dried foods, tinned foods, candles, lighter fluid, distilled water, solar batteries, everything his family might need, packed away in their basement. Lenny was perhaps the only person he'd met who understood this fear. She'd even said she felt it too, although for her it materialised differently, blossoming into an all-consuming fury at seemingly everything and everyone. As the only two residents left in his building, they'd become unlikely friends. He hadn't met anyone like Lenny before; she could be funny, even sweet, and was always incredibly sharp. He hadn't taken her rhetoric too seriously. Not back when he'd known her. It was something more like a joke. Irony sparkled in her eyes whenever she said and did outrageous things.

'White men,' Lenny told him, those eyes sparkling, 'that's who. White men have it hardest these days.'

She'd said this before taking him into her mouth and sucking earnestly. He exhaled. Granted, there were things you couldn't say anymore. Or do. He looked up at the ceiling, absently grabbing a fistful of her short hair. Relatively harmless things could really land you in it, that was true. But he'd had a decent run. No major scrapes. And besides, some of the things they'd got up to, back in the good years – well, it had all got a bit out of hand, hadn't it? He certainly wouldn't want his daughter involved in any of that. He looked down; Lenny's mascara-heavy lashes masked her eyes. Along her side parting, the hair looked soft, fine enough to see through to the scalp beneath. He cringed – why had he thought of his daughter? What the fuck was wrong with him? He tried to re-engage with the present scene; anticipating, more than feeling, the wet of Lenny's mouth, her cheeks – slack, then tensing – a smooth ridge of teeth – the tongue roving – all framed by smudged lipstick – up and down. He wove his fingers together at the base of her neck, closed his eyes, and relaxed into a rhythm.

When he finished, she smiled and excused herself to the en-suite, coming back fresher-faced a few minutes later. Even as she lay beside him on the crumpled bedsheets, Lenny's body was tense, seemingly primed for attack. So when, instead of launching into one of her diatribes, she asked for a favour, Richard readily agreed. With the world being as it was, so uncertain and fragile, he found himself moved to help her. He hadn't known then that Lenny was Jake's *mother*. That context arrived much later, along with a dawning sense of guilt: had he, however inadvertently, taken advantage of her?

After all, recast as the actions of a concerned parent, Lenny's sexual aggression made a certain kind of sad sense. People were complicated, yes, but perhaps the same loves and fears motivated them all. Until this strange disaster befell him, so much of his world had been screens of numbers. The tiniest deltas aggregated and integrated, projected and explained; sliced and diced then crushed into monochromatic charts and graphs, wrangled into decks and mulled over, signed off, submitted. And, of course, under the layers of bundling, tranching and repackaging, this was indeed the world. Everyone's individual choices: dreams and promises. Altogether, packaged up into funds, they amounted to a literal, collective hope for the future.

'Rich?'

Behind him, a light shone warm and honeyed into the dark. Claire, in her soft cardigan and slippers, leaning against the door, frowned at him with gentle concern.

'Rich' – she said his name like music, like magic. 'What are you doing out there?'

CARTMEL

People – and you'll notice this if you actually look at them. I mean really look. Pay attention to the people around you. Notice who they are; what they say and do. Take that woman over there, on my left, shovelling porridge into her mouth. Do you see it? I'll tell you what that is: ugliness. People are ugly. And stupid. Motivated only by fear or jealousy or, I don't know, occasional petty hatred. The internet simply offered a medium for all this crapola. It's the sad, inevitable consequence of semi-educating the masses. Granting every idiot the dizzying power of a spray can and wall. Take away the moderating effect of a physical body, all those humbling flaws, or of other people, the risk of social consequence, and – *voilà!* I noticed this ugliness a long time ago. I'm a fast learner, you must have figured that out by now. I understood how all this worked far sooner than most. Saw where we were headed. Even so, these last few weeks it's been getting to me. Maybe that's just a consequence of too much exposure; seeing so much of all these ugly people, living out their small and pointless lives. Last night, sitting in the dim lighting of the hotel room, I found myself returning to the same question: what's the point? All these words, all of my energy in service of . . . what?

Across the table, Rob nodded enthusiastically. He swallowed, then put down his fork. Dabbed his mouth with the edge of a napkin.

'Yes, well, exactly,' he said. 'And of course it's insights like those – that's why you're such a crucial voice, Lenny, for this moment.'

The lenses of his glasses were smudged, giving his eyes a misty, faraway look, despite his persistent grin. I could say anything to this twit; he was never actually listening. A defiant smear of yellow glistened across his chin. On his plate below, beside the toast and sausage, spilling into a syrupy sludge of beans, sat the remainder of his second fried egg. He beamed at me, lowering his voice to a conspiratorial hush.

'The rooms here are pretty plush, aren't they? I always say it's worth splashing out for a boutique hotel.'

That was a good one. Rob never splashed out for anything. Not for me, anyway, until the *Mail* bought serialisation rights for my new book. Funny, isn't it? How quickly everything changes. Back when Rob first read the manuscript, he'd flat-out refused to publish it.

'Why this sudden . . . change?' he'd whined, slumping back in his chair and fixing me with a plaintive stare.

Woke Capitalism: How Corporations Sold Out the Working Class lay on the table between us, at the time just a hefty wad of brilliant-white sheets. We were sitting in a bland conference room; he hadn't even bothered to book a restaurant for this 'editorial chat'.

'We have a winning formula with *No Mo' Woke*,' he'd gone on. 'There's so much more ground to cover in these woke wars. Your readers are depending on you to take up the cause. We need your writing now, more than ever. And we're behind you. The whole editorial team is so excited to see where you take the concept next! But this doesn't quite work for us,' he'd said, with a hand on the condemned manuscript. 'Let's go back to basics, hey? Stop trying to be Cohen with all this lofty "state of the nation" stuff. We're looking for something a bit more *accessible*.'

Rob had been pleased with *No Mo' Woke*'s performance. While it was true that very few copies had sold, the figures were in line with his modest expectations. Books like that weren't supposed to sell, not really. Low five figures were the best you could hope for. The book's success was measured in column inches. Its real audience was the media. Rob, after publishing (in a single year) two books on 'the climate emergency' and another described (horrifyingly) as 'Virginia Woolf meets *The Vagina Monologues*', needed to restore a semblance of balance to his list. He'd acquired my book with that goal in mind. Publishing *No Mo' Woke* definitively shoved his list back to the 'middle ground', the everyman's moral position. He'd wanted more of the same, but I'd had bigger ideas.

'No – *you* have a winning formula.' I'd jabbed an incensed index finger at him. 'I have a tired schtick. Don't bullshit me. Writing *No Mo' Woke 2* forces me into a corner. You know it does. I'm going where there's a future, where there's money. This is the book. And you're going to publish it.'

The meeting had been tense, unresolved. But the article

forced Rob's hand. He rushed the book to publication, hoping to surf the wave of notoriety-fuelled publicity to the best-seller list. And it worked: *Woke Capitalism* was a certified hit. The early controversy from the gold-bar saga snowballed into more coverage than money could buy. So of course Rob threw cash at it, plastering my grinning face across the sides of buses, on train platform posters and all over everybody's social media feeds. *The Secular Bible* was emblazoned on the book's jacket and repeated breathlessly across the media. I was booked onto TV news – those American-style discussion programmes that've taken over here – plus the radio shows. There I was on *Woman's Hour* and even the *Today* programme, hilariously. Everyone, especially those who didn't agree with me, wanted to hear what I had to say. Amplified everything I said.

And now that it had turned out so brilliantly, Rob was hardly going to challenge the notion that his razor-sharp insight had so transformed my career. He was more than happy to forget history and embrace my fictionalisation. The truth, more often than not, benefited from the techniques of fiction. Every hack knew that.

I sipped my burnt coffee and took in the room. The tinkle-and-scrape of the middle-aged middle classes stuffing their faces with complimentary cooked breakfasts. The oily-sweet stink of it repulsed me. I watched on as a woman across the room piloted a forkful of hash brown, sausage and grease into her open mouth. Unperturbed, Rob flipped through the festival programme.

'This fellow who's interviewing you today . . . Very interesting guy. One of Britain's brightest and best, apparently. A proper literary man.' Rob leaned back and eyed me. 'Much like myself,' he added.

When I didn't say anything to that, he frowned.

'You're ignoring me.'

'Piss off, Rob. I'm eating.'

He nodded pointedly at my empty place setting. 'You're not eating.'

Fair enough, I haven't eaten breakfast since late 2005. But I wanted to not-eat breakfast in peace and quiet contempt of the munching masses around me.

'Word to the wise, old girl,' he half-whispered, savouring the cheesy line. It was a nervous tic: he believed movie-style dialogue could shield him from the full gravity of whatever he was trying to say. 'This guy might be tricky. He's been making a bit of a name for himself, skewering a few sacred cows . . . Not that I'm worried about you.' He gave me an apologetic smile and little lines, like whiskers, appeared just above his cheeks. 'I know you can handle yourself. But, maybe, be careful with him. Okay?'

'Did you just call me an "old cow"? I hear that's considered workplace harassment these days.'

'Snowflake,' he retorted, laughing.

Indeed, Rob had much to be cheerful about. Doling out his three-star advice in a four-star hotel, he looked pleased as punch in a pale-pink shirt, buttoned to a few inches shy of his

117

throat. A quirky cardigan was slung over the chair behind him. And his hair, I noticed, no longer had those shocks of grey at the temples. He'd clearly embraced the caricature I'd created for him: bumbling, brilliant editorial wunderkind.

It was easy, in the wake of all this, to think of myself as some kind of master genius. Rob certainly did. I caught him sometimes, staring at me with a look of admiration that verged on blasphemy. But I was all too aware of the dangers of excessive self-aggrandisement. That was the curse of the ballsy nineties lady journo. To come from nothing, being a bit of an ugly duckling to boot, unremarkable at school, to literally getting paid two, three, four – even fucking five – quid a word. To men, twice your age, throwing money at you in the hope of a fuck or some words or just a bit of your sultry pouting. It changed something inside you, of course it did. The entire social system was upended when you realised just how valuable, just how marketable, your everyday thoughts were. Your young, willing body was. The wit and witticisms you'd been giving away for free, unappreciated, in whatever idiotic town you'd crawled out from. 'Course, you ended up developing a healthy dose of self-belief. As well you should. I did. My so-called contemporaries certainly did. But too much confidence could be dangerous. Especially now that we were no longer at the bleeding edge of things. I, at least, knew my own limitations.

'Excuse me, Lenny? Hello.'

A girl stepped up to our table. She was tall with a health-ful, sort of Dutch look: long hair brushed back into a bright and bouncing ponytail, wearing a neat shirt and slacks, bland-ly smart-casual as an event photographer.

'I'm Amanda. I'm here to take you to the site for your appointments. This is' – she handed me a bright folio stuffed with papers – 'your itinerary. It's got absolutely everything you need to know about the festival. And here' – she licked a finger and leafed through a few pages – 'are my contact details. If you need anything at all during your time here, just call me. Day or night, I'm here to help.'

Rob jumped up to shake the girl's hand.

'Excellent, yes. Right. Lenny's all set to go.'

'Go where? My talk isn't until five – it's barely noon.'

With his wide smile tightening to a grimace, Rob reminded me about an apparently prescheduled meeting with the festi-val's director, Catherine Livesey.

'And we were thrilled at the invitation,' he added, presum-ably for Amanda's benefit.

Obligingly, I stood and brushed the wrinkles out of my trousers.

'Alright then.'

Declining the colourful 'festival tote', I stuffed the fold-er into my regular old handbag. I tossed my phone in too, ignoring its stack of unread messages. Those could wait. Leaving Rob behind, I followed the girl out of the musty dining room, through the carpeted corridor and lobby, past the reception desk and down the hotel's front steps into the damp sunshine.

'I read in an interview that you enjoy exercising,' she said as we stood on the precipice of the hotel's lawns and gravel drive. 'So I didn't book a minicab. I thought we could walk instead. It'll only take about half an hour. It's a very charming country walk. And we'll see some of the sights in town. But we can still call a cab if you prefer.'

The words rushed out in a bout of nervous professionalism. Squinting into the distance, the gentle hills did look rather green and pleasant. Nice, if you went in for that sort of thing. I could understand why the poets exalted all this in verse. And why we hacks churned out prose in defence of its borders. So off we went, crunching down the driveway and onto a snaking country road. There was no pavement; instead we walked single-file along the hedgerow. Dense tufts of foliage and jutting branches crowded our path, obscuring the view. It was disconcerting. At any moment a car could come flying around the bend and knock us flat. Amanda didn't seem to mind one bit, frequently twisting her neck to address me, going on about various underwhelming local items of interest.

'I was really glad' – a rustling wind interrupted her like static – 'I mean, so excited to be your liaison.' Amanda turned again to grin at me, her ponytail flicking madly across her face. 'Actually, I'm a big fan of yours.' I nodded, preoccupied with how little attention she was paying to the road ahead. 'Your story is so inspirational and – I hope you don't mind me saying – but I think we're quite similar, actually.'

'That's nice.' I gave her a conciliatory nod and smile, before waving her back towards the direction of oncoming traffic.

She changed the topic, pointing to what were apparently racehorse stables, somewhere over to our right. I was relieved when at last we turned off the road, passing through a small farm gate into an overgrown field.

'This is a bit of a shortcut,' Amanda said after latching the gate behind us. We followed a path trodden into the tall, yellowing grass. 'It's private land, technically, but everyone comes through here. The owner doesn't mind. He's a friend of the festival. That's it up ahead, by the way.' She pointed towards a white blur in the middle distance. 'Those tents are the main venues, and see the little stone building? That's Clifford House where— *Oh!*'

Amanda clasped her hands to her mouth, eyes wide. An insistent tug at my elbow jerked me backwards, twisting my shoulder. Uselessly, my mind grasped at rationalisations. I heard panting. Heavy, laboured breaths scoured through my confusion. *I was being attacked.* My hands squeezed into fists. Stumbling, but unafraid, I turned to stare down my assailant: a mass of wild hair, shambolic clothing and lifelong unaccountability.

Jake.

'Mum—' He cracked open like a bottomless void.

I yanked myself free. 'Get away from me.'

121

My voice was blunt and forceful. Amanda, behind us, gasped again. In Jake's quick, darting eyes, I saw caution. Fear. At least he was still capable of that, not as reduced to wild recklessness as his unkempt appearance suggested. He attempted another step towards me, but I shook my head and mouthed a single word: *No*. He squeezed his eyes shut and pulled at his sleeves. Then put his hands to his ears and grimaced. Utterly pathetic.

'Fuck off,' I spat.

After another few seconds of agonised consideration, he did indeed fuck off, beginning a creeping retreat back through the grass. My pulse thudded hard against my chest and neck and temples.

Jake had been threatening something along these lines for weeks now, via texts of escalating frequency and lunacy. Mostly semi-coherent lower-case whingeing peppered with emojis. Between complaints of neglect and exploitation, he'd made repeated demands to see me. To talk to me. Eventually the demands had blossomed into outright threats. Not that I'd expected him to actually follow through. Planning an ambush, booking a train ticket . . . It was more than I'd thought him capable of. Then again, even babies eventually manage their first few steps unaided. And in any case, it all came to nothing, as per usual. He was too afraid to squeak more than a single, infantile word.

'Shouldn't we help him?' Amanda asked, hovering at my side.

'He's fine,' I snapped.

Amanda looked from me to Jake's receding figure, uncertain of where her responsibilities lay. This particular situation wasn't, I supposed, covered in the information pack.

'Maybe we should catch up with him' – she spoke in a small, strained voice – 'check if he's okay . . .'

I said nothing to that. When, finally, Jake reached the gate and shuffled back through it, I turned and began again towards the festival.

'Please,' said Amanda, 'can we just . . . Lenny, I really think—'

'We're done with this conversation.'

Mercifully, Amanda shut up after that. Without her incessant chatter, only the rustling crunch underfoot marked our progress. Grateful for the relative silence, I puffed out a deep breath. I'd send Jake more money later, of course. I wasn't a monster. But he couldn't have my time. Especially not now, not here.

'Miriam!'

Catherine Livesey, a woman in her forties still trying to come off as precocious, met us at the steps of Clifford House with her arms flung open in a ludicrous welcome gesture. After shepherding us inside the vast, wood-panelled entrance hall, she guided us deeper into the building, dancing up a flight of wide stairs and across the landing to an imposing pair of carved doors. Here, she dismissed Amanda with a bright and pointed 'Thank you.' Inside her office, two huge bay windows washed the room in early-afternoon light. A spread of fruit and charcuterie was laid out, along with a slender glass jug of, presumably, water.

'Don't worry.' She took a decanter out from a cabinet and held it up by the neck. It was the old-fashioned crystal type. The sort of thing your nan might coo over at a car boot sale. 'I know you like a drop of the good stuff.'

As she poured, I looked around the room. I had to admit it was a nice office. An overbearing, impressively empty mahogany desk dominated the space; tellingly, there was no computer in sight. Our luncheon spread was marooned a few feet away, on a smaller side table covered with a stiff white cloth. Floating shelves of books adorned the walls, like oversized art.

'What's your take on the "diversity question"?' said Catherine, holding a glass out to me.

I accepted the drink without an answer. She gave me a coquettish smile, peering up through the dark strands of her fringe.

'I thought it might do as a sort of unofficial theme for this year's festival. A rallying cry of sorts. It's one of those patterns that appeals to the human brain, isn't it? The *such-and-such* question . . .' She sank into an armchair, gesturing for me to do the same. 'Like Beethoven's fate motif or those ridiculous frogs. It's a meme. And a useful shorthand for, well, the question at hand. What is, I truly believe, the most important question of our time in many ways . . . But do be frank, Miriam, please. What do *you* make of the idea?'

I sniffed at the drink – it was sherry; of course it was sherry. Nonetheless, I closed my eyes and pursed my lips around the glass's smooth edge. Those first few sips, which I always take exceptionally slowly, ushered in a familiar flush. Softly, I reopened my eyes. I welcomed the tingling expansion of capillaries in my cheeks and lips; felt my pulse fluttering with anticipatory glee. I looked down at the glass, then swished the syrupy liquid around a little. Why did I like drinking so much? I couldn't stand being drunk. Though total sobriety was arguably worse. It was the in-between land that I liked. The place where my ideas were sharp and the world was blurry and its inhabitants seemed further away, less stupid and hideous . . .

Catherine watched me, uncomfortable in the silence following her little speech. She wasn't expecting it. People like me weren't exactly known for quiet contemplation. But what was there to say? Maybe she had a point. The problem was that she was just so exhausting. Too much earnest need bundled up in painfully deliberate middle-class tics. I mean, who kept a decanter of sherry in their office? Seriously? Suppressing a headshake, I took another sip. It was better to embrace your rougher edges, I reckoned. Play up your dropped t's and h's, squashed vowels and coarse language. Show total irreverence towards the old guard's good breeding.

'Look, Miriam—'

'It's Lenny.'

'Of course, yes. Lenny. Look, let's be frank. I know what you're thinking. You've been around for yonks, but we've never come calling before. I'll hold up my hands and apologise for that. We should have had you here for *No Mo' Woke*. That was my oversight.'

Swirling my drink again, I let the apology pass unacknowledged.

'Honestly, back then, I thought you were a bit, well, *coarse* for our crowd. But that was my mistake. The times are changing – you know that. I think you understand that better than most. It isn't easy, not these days, to entice people to pay for the privilege of sitting in a tent and watching backbench MPs pontificate . . . That's maybe too facetious.' She flashed me a practised, guilty smile. 'I still believe, deeply, that the sort of cultural smorgasbord we offer here at Cartmel is vitally important. More so now than in the good times, I'd argue. Crucially, though, we've got to acknowledge what people are going through. We must appeal to the "squeezed middle". And who better, Lenny, to speak to that demographic than you?'

'Is that so?'

'You know it is,' she beamed, hopeful that I was finally thawing with her change of tack. 'I'll admit, I don't quite know how you managed it, but you've pulled off something remarkable. *Woke Capitalism* is genius. Reading you, people feel seen, yet you allow them to remain at arm's length from

126

that very feeling. You take all this resentment' – she mimed rubbing a substance between her thumbs and fingertips, then released it into the air like confetti – 'and make it *righteous*. Your readers come away believing they're aggrieved on someone else's behalf. I'll say it again: genius. Powerful stuff. I mean, you wouldn't believe the buzz on our socials when we announced you as a speaker. The event's completely sold out.'

I allowed myself a small smile at that. Talk was fine, but bums-in-seats? Those were incontrovertible. Pressing her hands together, Catherine grinned back at me. Satisfied that she'd won me over with this burst of outright flattery. Through the windows behind her, I watched a few hazy figures amble across the grass like grazing cows.

'Stunning grounds, aren't they? So much history.' Catherine let out a wistful sigh. 'We're the UK's oldest cultural festival. Did you know that? I know Cheltenham like to think they are, but we outdate them by three years, actually. That's why tradition, and preservation, are so important to us here. And why it's vital that we don't bow to popular fads. There's so much pressure these days to *modernise*. We're constantly being told to invite new voices, shake things up, appeal to diverse audiences . . . Apparently that's what it takes to survive now. Some of the other festivals have already caved, as you've no doubt noticed. Well, I don't care if it makes me unpopular, I won't do it.' She tapped a small, emphatic fist against her open palm. The motion became petulant in her birdlike hands. 'I simply won't. We're going to go on as we always have: bringing the very best of British thinkers together in one place. And of course, Lenny, no such gathering would be complete without you. Well. I'm so glad we squeezed in a little time to get properly acquainted. I'm sure this is the beginning of a great friendship between us.'

She stood with a stilted formalism that signalled the end of our tête-à-tête. Neither of us had touched the food and I wondered how long it would sit there. Maybe she had an entire afternoon of identical meetings planned, all playing out beside these same platters. How many times had unwashed hands, I wondered, fingered those slices of meat? Rearranged the little pieces of cheese and fruit? While Catherine prattled on about 'friendship' with her persistent, insipid smile. We weren't friends. Two years ago, I doubt she'd have deigned to piss my way if I were on fire. And if she didn't think I could shift books and tickets, she still wouldn't give me the time of day. Catherine was a pragmatist, though, and I was the lesser of two evils. Following her lead, I eased up to standing. She clasped my free hand in both of hers.

'Please do think of Cartmel as your home – and, I hope, a resoundingly clear answer to the diversity question!'

'Speakers' Tent.' Could there be two less appealing words to describe a location? It promised a tireless and tiring assault on the ears and mind: people paid to speak, all speaking simultaneously, in a desperate bid for relevance. I decided to skip it, ignoring Amanda's assurances that I would be welcomed into the so-called 'VIP area'. That was practically guaranteed to be a menagerie of grotesques, puffed up with obnoxious self-regard. Instead, I told Amanda to find a place where we could get a drink. Naturally, the nearest option was a wanky gastropub. The drinks weren't far off London prices. But it felt good to get away from the artificial chumminess of the festival for a while. Pubs were much the same everywhere, weren't they? A bar, some tables, a TV and a few old gits in the corner. The sticky, sour smell of spilt booze.

'So. You're a student?'

We had a booth to ourselves near the back. Amanda swallowed a minuscule sip of her half-pint before answering. She seemed uncomfortable with our deviation from the festival schedule but, to her credit, hadn't complained.

'Politics.'

'And what's the plan for after?'

'I'm not sure. Maybe journalism.'

I gave a bitter laugh. The idea of a young person choosing this industry was absurd. Didn't she realise that the good times were pretty much over? These days, unless you were the daughter of a baron LARPing as relatably middle class, our trade didn't have much to offer. Did she fancy exploiting herself for pennies per word, grinding out culture war fodder and outrage bait with zero scope for flair or individuality? As a freelancer, mind you. Cheap, commodity labour,

129

temporarily serving the algorithm that would one day replace her entirely.

That was the way things were going. It'd all seemed so innocuous at first. The net was just something for the boffins to fiddle about with. Children running companies with ridiculous-sounding names. Who could be afraid of anything called Yahoo, AltaVista . . . Google? Imagine having a major component of your industry destroyed by some bloke called Craig and his sodding 'list'. It beggared belief. Prime newspaper real estate depreciated into a ghetto of online advertising and cheap sponsored content. No more sellers' market for a couple inches of sombre ad copy. Now we got fractions of a penny for a full-colour advert flashing garishly above the line. Whatever 'the line' meant in this digital dystopia. If I were Amanda, with a degree under my belt and a long life ahead of me, I'd be getting into tech.

'Do you agree with my politics?'

'Not entirely, no. But I admire you – really. I think your evolution over the years into the figure you are today has been incredible. I mean it,' she said, protesting my snorted scepticism. 'I'm writing about you in my dissertation, actually. I think you're part of a cohort of women spearheading a new style of political discourse. You, Jess Phillips, Angela Rayner, Penny Mordaunt . . . even Liz Truss. I have tons of admiration for all of you. Actually—' She hesitated. 'I was hoping to ask you something.'

'Go on, then.'

'Okay.' Amanda puffed her cheeks. 'Right, so. How did you *know?*'

I made a face.

'I mean, how did you know that everything would work out like this? Your move from the *Telegraph* to the *Observer*, right when that *Alazon* piece was going viral. And then the book, and your new message, resonating with so much of the country. All of it. Did you have, I don't know . . .' Her smile was self-conscious, disarming. The kind of smile smart women learn when they're young. '. . . some sort of masterplan all along?'

A fair question, but the wrong one. It wasn't about knowing. It was impossible to ever know whether a thing would go one way or another. Our world was chaotic. Even the so-called experts and their supercomputers couldn't predict the trajectory of a bouncing pinball. I've never pretended to *know* any better. Instead, I've relied on my instincts over the years. Research, preparation, and all that, had a place. But ultimately, you had to trust your fingers to push the right buttons on the machine.

'I didn't have any special knowledge. I just saw an opportunity. That's all it ever comes down to. When you spot your chance, fucking go for it. Force your way in. Bully, flatter, call in favours. Do whatever it takes.'

'But what if you can't, what if no one owes you any favours or—'

'Remember' – the sincerity in my voice surprised me

131

– 'you've always got your words. Even when you're at a disadvantage, what you say and write can completely turn things around. You said it yourself. A new style of discourse, right? Language is your interface to this world, Amanda. Words are your weapons, they're your tools, your currency.'

I shrugged and rubbed at my elbow. Amanda didn't look convinced. Not that I expected her to understand. Most people couldn't. I just had a different way of assessing situations. When my perennial fuck-up of a son came back from that farm crying murder, I recognised the *potential*. His mess had the makings of a story – perfect for triggering the online content machine into action. The timing couldn't have been better. I needed a soft rebrand before moving papers. It was chance to address a few of my old controversies, while drumming up enough fresh drama to guarantee eyeballs on the new column. With any luck, the renewed interest would bring Rob back and all. So I went for it. I dusted off my keyboard and got to work; sent a new ball spinning out towards the pins.

'Are you really saying' – a frown crinkled Amanda's otherwise smooth forehead – 'that it's just luck and . . . opportunism?'

'Does that disappoint you?'

'No, it's not that' – she waved the accusation away. 'It's just a lot. I need to think about it.'

Neither of us spoke for a while. Beaded condensation trickled down Amanda's glass, dampening the napkin beneath.

To its right, my phone blinked with a flurry of new messages. Jake. Again. Irritation surged through my sinuses, ached behind my eyes. His antics were the last thing I needed right now. But clearly, an hour or two of peace was too much to hope for. He was incapable of taking care of himself for more than five fucking minutes.

I pressed my fingertips to my temples, closed my eyes, and exhaled.

It was fair to say that some people deserved their place here more than others. Besides the namby-pamby types who 'don't agree with borders', we've all accepted that implicitly. *That* was what having a country meant. So there was no point in shying away from the real question: who actually deserved to be here? Who deserved England?

Put like that, it sounded ugly. Nothing like Catherine's cutesy construction. Still, it remained an old favourite in my industry. Trotted out under one guise or another to stir up outrage, patriotism or even pity. Most of my colleagues were too cowardly to engage with the question's full implications. Too squeamish to venture beyond the easy, clear-cut examples. Not me. Self-delusion was a stupefying comfort: I'd rather face up to the truth. *My son didn't deserve his place.* The admission deflated me. It violated all of my evolutionary and cultural impulses. And left me doubting my vocation – weren't we all fighting to preserve this country for our children? Week after week, in print and pixels, advocating on behalf of their futures? In reality, Jake was unworthy of such efforts.

That was the stone-cold truth. Why should I judge him any more leniently than a young migrant clinging to a dinghy? My son was a failure, and a drain on our society.

The phone was flashing insistently when I blinked my eyes back open. A call this time. I looked up towards Amanda's concerned expression.

'Think I should I answer that?'

'No,' she said immediately. At my raised eyebrow, she rushed to explain. 'It's just, I've got to get you on stage in twenty minutes. And he might need a bit more time than that. How about we find him afterwards and—'

'So you're telling me to mug him off?'

'For the next few hours, please.' She pressed her hands together in mock-supplication. After a cautious pause, she began again. 'Lenny . . .' Her voice was steady, determined. 'Weren't we done with this conversation?'

I laughed – genuinely surprised by Amanda's flash of audacity. It was refreshing to finally encounter a person with a bit of gumption, a bit of resilience. Who had an actual fucking sense of humour. Of course, she was just trying to do her job, appealing to my ego in the hope of keeping proceedings on schedule. But that in itself was a sign of intelligent life. She knew when to kiss up and, crucially, how to push back. Somewhat cheered, I turned off my phone and downed the rest of my whisky.

'Come on, then, drink up.' I drummed the tabletop. 'It's almost showtime.'

SHOWTIME

Backstage, it's sparse and perfunctory. Floors and walls painted black. The tables and chairs look like the sort you'd find in a school. A curtain-lined passage leads off to the stage. Though slightly muffled, the sound of Catherine's introductory speech dominates, seeming to bounce around the walls. Staff dressed in black with headsets and clipboards are positioned about the room, occasionally whispering to one another. On my arrival, a technician leaps into action, steadying my shoulders with unexpected tenderness as he hooks a headset over my ears. He adjusts a Barbie-flesh-toned ball by its quivering wire until it sits an inch from my lips. I lift the side of my top, allowing access to my waistband, where he clips in the power unit. Then he gives me a thumbs-up.

'Three minutes.'

My young interviewer is surprisingly bashful during his turn. His arms flap impotently as an identical headset is adjusted around his ears. He decides to slip the main unit into a trouser pocket, rather than submit to further attentions from the technician. It's then that I notice the strangeness of his ensemble: a chunky-knit jumper layered over a crumpled blue shirt, the untucked edges peeking out beneath and – I shake my head in appalled disbelief – *sports shoes*? He gathers up a messy stack of papers now: printouts, magazines and such. He tucks the lot under his arm and smiles at me, apologetically. The overall effect is startlingly similar to Rodge. We're directed to stand side by side at the stage entrance as Catherine, delighting in her role as emcee, begins our introductions with gushing enthusiasm.

'. . . so thrilled to introduce you to our first event of the festival. It will be, I'm sure, a deep and fascinating discussion between two very important British thinkers, on what I hope is a wide range of topics about the future of our great country. First, Martin Bass. Martin is perhaps Britain's foremost man of letters. He is a critic at *Perspective!* magazine, and his fresh, insightful writing has been featured absolutely everywhere – including the *LRB*, the *New Yorker* and *HQ* magazine, to name just a few. Today, Martin will be speaking with Lenny Leonard about her landmark new book, *Woke Capitalism: How Corporations Sold Out the Working Class*. Now, this book is really something special. I don't say that lightly. An instant *Sunday Times* bestseller, it was shortlisted for the Orwell Prize and is being celebrated by many as "the secular Bible". After a few moments with Lenny, I'm sure you'll see why it's merited such buzz. She's really one of the most forward-thinking intellectuals of our time, a real champion of working-class Brits and – I'm pleased to say – a dear friend of mine. Now then. Without further ado, it's my huge honour to welcome Lenny and Martin to Cartmel!'

And so we walk out from the negative into the bright lights, into the warm pool of receptive applause, and take our respective places. I perch on a velvet wing chair while Martin slides onto a stiff-looking Chesterfield. There's a rug laid out, along with plants and a lamp, all very stylishly staged. A low table between us bears two empty tumblers and a jug of ice water. The effect of this little 'set' is striking, underscoring the artifice of the entire construct. Cables run along the edge of the stage area, where a small screen marks the time in ominous red digits. Above our heads a huge television displays a live recording of the scene. On screen, I watch Martin fold his right leg over his left, giving himself the look of a single-stroke number four. It cuts to a close-up of me, looking up at myself. Grinning, I give her a big thumbs-up. A rumble of laughter pads out the fading applause.

'Ar-uhm, er. Hello,' Martin says.

The milky darkness of the audience responds ambiguously. In a little of the theatre I'm so known for, I produce a small metallic flask, unscrew the top and pour its contents into my tumbler. The audience – that tricksy, colossal organism – seems to gasp and chuckle in response. A norm has been broken; it sets a tone of unpredictability. With a broad smile and nod, I toast to the audience and take a performative sip from the glass. A lone whoop rings from the back of the room.

'Well,' the young interviewer begins again. 'Well, that's quite the beginning to proceedings. I, ah, might be needing one of those by the end. Ha ha ha. So, erm, Lenny. It's good to be up here with you. Thanks to Cathy, we know a bit about who you are now. But perhaps it would be nice to hear you introduce your work in your own words. One thing about your new book is that it's hard to place. It's quasi-evangelical and not at all, really, what one would expect from a journalist's book. Who is *Woke Capitalism* for?'

He leans back and stretches out his legs, literally reclining as I answer his bullshit question. Obviously not listening. I don't bother with looking at him, instead directing my comments out into the dark. You do feel so marooned up on a stage; especially one as large and temporary as this. There's a strange tension between the physical heft of the structure – after all, it's a fuck-off big tent, powered by a special electricity line from the main grid – and its impermanence. In a couple of weeks this entire space will be dismantled, packed down into trucks and driven away. While it's here, though, it's magical, isn't it? How else can you unite five hundred people into a single, invisible force?

My interviewer continues nodding, long after I stop speaking.

'Would you say, then, that this book shares some DNA with the kiss-and-tell memoir?' He gives me a shifty smile. 'After all, you only started to write about your impressions of capitalism after a, uh, shall we say *liaison* of sorts with your neighbour.'

I suppose he thinks I'll be embarrassed by that. Easily shamed. Pah. Over at *Perspective!* they know a thing or two about wanking off bankers in the name of journalism. You'd be hard pressed to find any criticism of their owners' financiers within the magazine's pages.

'It's true, I shagged a banker.' My words are slow and unemotional. 'And I found out a thing or two about what's going on in this country.'

'Like what?'

'As detailed in the book' – I gesture towards it with a knuckle – 'there's a huge demographic shift going on within the offices of many banks, tech companies, engineering firms, all those sorts of places. Most of us have no idea of what's going on in those firms, and while we've been distracted they've handed out jobs very unfairly. And these are good jobs, by the way. We're talking six-figure salaries, cushy benefits and lots of perks. Do we really want these jobs handed out to people on the basis of woke politics? Without getting to hear about all this first-hand, I'd never have imagined the extent of it. I believe I had a responsibility to report on what I found.'

'Sleeping with the, ah . . . enemy, in effect?'

'I would've thought you were above puerile jabs and pearl-clutching. This is serious. You yourself, Martin, have written about the disappearing middle class.' His eyebrows rise in soft surprise. He didn't expect me to do my homework. 'This demographic shift is the cause. When young people from middle- and working-class backgrounds are excluded from some of the best work opportunities on offer, of course they aren't able to build lives for themselves. And we can't sit around waiting for the banks and tech companies to do the right thing, to fix this problem. Of course they won't. We need regulatory scrutiny. We need to demand that this new workforce reflects the demographics of the entire United Kingdom. Not just "multicultural" London.'

He sits back, letting my brief pause pool into a silence.

'We should,' I press on, 'be curious about the people who wield power in our lives. And we should have visibility into who those people are, and what they're up to. This isn't limited to a particular industry. Once an institution gives you power, whether that institution is tech or finance or medical research, it's possible to move into power in almost any other domain. This isn't theoretical, mind you. We do in fact have a banker as a prime minister right now. And one who illustrates exactly what I mean about the distribution of these jobs, and where the consequences lead.'

'You have a problem with our prime minister?'

'I didn't say that. What I'm pointing out is that the leadership in our country is in a unique situation. Unique within Europe, in any case. If you look at the leadership of our country, the top jobs and the cabinets, you'll see a phenomenon that's completely different from any other European country. We're much closer to America, in that respect, and of course—'

'I'm afraid this is all getting a bit theoretical' – he cuts me off bluntly. 'Perhaps you could elaborate a bit. What's so, um, different about British and American political leaders, compared to those in Europe?'

'Demographics. You can see it at a glance.'

'I see. You're talking about race?'

'That's part of it, yes.'

'But, and forgive me if I'm being . . .' He sifts the air with his hands. Finally, at least, sitting up properly. 'Er, maybe I'm a bit slow. But what does this have to do with banks?'

Usually, they at least read the introduction of the book. Whatever, I'll spell it out for him if I must.

'The fastest-growing sectors of our economy are disproportionately hiring and promoting minority workers. This has been going on for years, but we're just now seeing the consequences. We're seeing the beginnings of a new social demographic in the UK with sizeable purchasing power. Corporations notice this, and pander to these new potential customers. That's what I mean by "woke capitalism". And of course these newly moneyed minorities are making political inroads too. Until recently, this was mostly visible at relatively low levels of governments. But now? Well, just take a look at the top political jobs in Britain. I'd say it's more extreme here than in America, even.'

'I see. And you believe that Europe is not experiencing this phenomenon?'

'No.'

'Why not?'

The audience has been very quiet during this exchange. It's a hard sell. People love the book, they love *Lenny*: the cavalier tell-it-as-it-is brashness. But when it gets to the substance,

143

my real message, that's when eyes glaze over and yawns need to be stifled. They want me to return to the hits, woke this and cancelled that. It's a strange thing, to achieve success and adoration, but without any real understanding. I'm like poor old Cassandra.

'We didn't notice that the "myth" of meritocracy was turning into a curse. What I mean is that the rhetoric we've used in this country over the past few decades has had unintended consequences. We told people to pull themselves up by their bootstraps, to work hard and earn their place in this country. And they did, in a strange and twisted way. With the help of quotas and affirmative action . . . they did. Most of the major European countries had different messaging for their minorities – I believe the technical term for their strategy was "fuck off back where you came from".' This aside elicits a relieved titter from the crowd. 'And indeed, that strategy seems to have worked better. While those countries may face issues from a resentful and disenfranchised minority underclass, they are not in any danger of their corporate or political spheres becoming woke. Their offices look the same as ours did in the eighties.

'In fact' – I throw a cheeky grin to the audience – 'I tried to advise camp Remain on exactly that strategy. "Just print pictures of our parliament and theirs," I told 'em. Ask the voters who they'd rather be governed by, and aligned with.' A rueful chuckle meets that image, as always. 'As you know,' I explain softly to Martin, 'I very much wanted to remain in the EU. I think my strategy would have done it!

'Anyway, that's enough politics talk for now. Let's move on. What I really care about is the personal. I care about the impact this is having on British families. We need to stop playing politics and focus on the personal. It's—'

'And what exactly' – he tilts a sports-shoe-clad foot in my direction as he interjects – 'is the difference between the personal and the political? Where does one draw the line?'

Well, that's obvious. I gently shake my head. The personal is anything that affects me. Everything else is political. And identity politics is whatever affects *you*, but not me. This heuristic has never led me astray. Of course, I don't actually say this. Instead, I pinch my brow into a concerned frown and speak from the heart.

'You know, it's sad that you need to ask that, Martin. It's sad that we as a society ended up so confused about the difference. Your generation can't put politics aside, ever, and your question explains exactly why that is. You are completely incapable of separating real life from politics.'

I turn from the young interviewer now, and squint up into the audience's dark void.

'But we know the difference, don't we? We know how to be compassionate towards each other, how to respect our social fabric. Working families, small communities, traditional British industries and jobs. We used to *value* those things.' I keep upping the rhetorical ante, playing the hits as a smattering of claps crescendos into applause. 'London's corrupting influence, all those woke corporations and liberal loonies, keep up their barrage of misinformation and misdirection and confusion—'

With a shrug and a smile, I wait out the audience's enthusiastic endorsement.

'We know the difference,' I add once it's quiet again. The big screens are, I'm sure, showing a close-up of my face. Those signature red lips smiling, with undeniably genuine warmth, as I turn my gaze back to the young interviewer.

'Sounds compelling, but aren't you just regurgitating cheap populism?'

There it is, his first real jab.

'A lot to "unpack" there' – a small, predictable titter at the appearance of my air quotes – 'but it sounds to me like what you're saying is that anything that resonates with a majority is by definition lowbrow or "populist"? Well, I call bullshit on that. That's typical elitist snobbery. I don't think there's anything wrong with calling a spade a . . .' I pause to cast a wry smile across the room. 'A piece of gardening equipment. And if lots of people like that message? More power to them.'

'Well, this is what I mean. That spade comment – aren't you just courting shock value?'

'Who's shocked?'

'Well, it's provocative language.'

'I don't accept that. Look, we've got to stop with the self-policing. We're so busy apologising for ancient history and imagined offences that we're losing our economic edge. I can guarantee you that China's not worrying about spades.'

He smiles and shakes his head, conceding the point.

'Alright then, Lenny.' He claps his hands together and a slip of paper falls from his lap to the floor, ignored. 'Let's get personal. For starters, your husband—'

'I'm not married.'

'Excuse me, your partner, Rodger Walters. He's a well-known, if somewhat controversial, professor of . . . European history?'

I give a slight nod.

'Already, that's a bit of a loaded term, isn't it? Well, your tumultuous relationship has played out in public after that explosive feature last year launched you to a new level of . . . uh, renown.' He steals a glance at me before carrying on. 'There's been some criticism of your behaviour towards Walters, with some even saying – and this is a quote from the *New Statesman* – that you "glorify domestic abuse and girl-boss misandry". What would you say, then, to those who criticise your conduct?'

With an air of heavy gravity, I nod slowly and begin my PR response. I don't mind this question one bit; in fact I like it. A reputation as a slight misandrist does me a whole lot of good. Just as often, I've been accused of misogyny, along with just about every -ism that's going these days. If anything, I'm a misanthrope. An equal-opportunity hater. Still, I'm read by women who've spent most of their lives being pushed about, forced to be homemakers *and* have jobs. Who've spent years cleaning up after ungrateful husbands and useless children

147

at the start and end of every workday. Many of them even experienced domestic abuse themselves, back when it was just known as 'marriage'. And suddenly, before their eyes, they went from silent workhorses to abominable 'Karens', blamed for all of the world's ills . . . including, somehow, their husbands' midlife crises. Even if they don't feel comfortable admitting it, most of them are secretly, vicariously, satisfied by how I treat Rodge. They see through my 'sincere and heartfelt apologies' for my 'completely unacceptable behaviour'. And they approve.

Besides, Rodge himself doesn't mind. He knows what I am and he knows that I'm worth it. I say the things he's terrified to say. I fight the battles he shies away from. If anything, his opinions are more hardline than mine. Even to me, some of his views are a tad extreme. But his few forays into 'free speech' with his undergraduate classes went badly enough to leave him fearful. Resentful. To a man afraid of voicing his own convictions, the occasional explosive fight is well worth the feeling of finally being heard.

'And he's now the director of a men's mental health charity, I understand?'

'Yes, and they've been doing wonderful work. I'm glad that this negativity has been transformed into something positive.'

Polite applause follows and Martin, too, claps softly along.

'Listening to you this evening, Lenny, it's not very, ah, clear where one should place you, politically speaking. Yes to Europe, no to multiculturalism, maybe a yes to feminism?

Pro-regulation, anti-affirmative action, pro-levelling up . . . It all comes off a little, hm, a little muddled. Though I'm sure there's rhyme and reason behind the apparent madness. All that to say, your shift to the left-leaning side of the British media was rather unexpected. Could you walk us through what you were thinking?'

We have such an outdated imagining of our media in this country. Left and right wing are obsolete concepts. They're different brands slapped onto a white-labelled product. We all seek clicks, and are simply following different strategies to achieve those clicks – that *attention*. Our motivation is to maximise our own profits, influence and longevity.

Back when I started out, the rags wooed potential buyers with baubles – free CDs, packets of seeds, glossy photos of Princess Di, et cetera. A simpler time. These days, when it comes to the strategic income stream, the picture is complicated. Online subscribers. We get 'em by telling 'em what they want to hear. Yes, we can challenge and even offend, but only in the ways they want to be offended and challenged. We all want to be a little bit offended, don't we? We like the thrill of falling, from the relative safety of a rollercoaster car. At first, it doesn't look too different from the 'free gift' of the nineties. A little sweetener to secure the sale. It's much more than that, though. The shift from serving advertisers to satisfying subscribers changes everything. Now you pay for us because you like hearing what we say, and believing that it's true. Yes, you do. You can get news anywhere online, for free.

But we're different. We tell you what you want to hear, while convincing you that it's the truth, told as close to objectively as possible.

'I don't consider it a leftist paper, actually—'

'Come on, now, you write for the *Observer*. You probably share a printer with Guardianistas. How can you call it anything else?'

'Well, if you'll let me finish . . .' A disapproving murmur buzzes softly. He's rude, and brash. Forgetting that it doesn't do to keep interrupting a nice, older lady. I'm not some young activist that he can bully and push around.

'Here's the thing. Monday to Saturday, you're right. The daily paper pumps out manufactured liberal-leaning rage bait. But read the comments, and you'll understand who the readership really is. How fed up they are. How tired they are of being berated for non-existent "privileges". By Sunday, they're in a frenzy. They're ready for church. That's where I come in, me and my colleagues. We put the week's nonsense into perspective, with considered, level-headed takes. Really, I'm just a common-sensist.' I laugh along with the frothy approval this garners. 'Yes, common sense. Something that's been sorely lacking in our media of late.'

It's an ingenious set-up: spanning both sides of the political debate, so that your readership is alternately enraged and soothed. Plausible deniability is right there if you need it, whenever you veer too far one way or the other. This strategy seems to engage subscribers more than simply sticking to one side. Our paper's read in Third World countries on cheap Android phones with low-data plans; it's read on iPads and MacBooks in student common rooms. Political leaders read it. Activists read it. People who don't read the news read it, one way or another. It has massive reach. Online, the paper's various social accounts 'share' continually, stirring up the hate and debate with provocative headlines, driving more traffic to our advertisers. And all this is backed, mind you, by a billion-pound war chest. That's right. While we come to you with a begging bowl, the for-profit limited liability company that owns these media properties is sitting on over a billion pounds of assets. With an explicit mandate to *secure its own continuity by renewing its membership and by dealing with threats to its existence.* Yeah, I think I picked the winning team.

'Your, ah, perspective certainly seems to have met a warm welcome. *Woke Capitalism* has created, without exaggeration, a media sensation. Raising your . . . your standing, I suppose, phenomenally. As a matter of fact, you were profiled in the *New Yorker* recently.'

From the messy pile, he produces an actual copy of the issue, which he then holds up, preposterously, to the audience.

'*Britain's unreasonable voice of reason* – there's the headline.'

'That's right,' I say, listening as he reads out the first few sentences.

'Well, what do you make of the media's response to you?'

'I've been on the outside for a long time, you know. Probably since before you were born.' A soft, predictable chuckle.

'And I think that spending so much time outside of the Fleet Street bubble has allowed me to remain closer to my roots. You hear how I speak. I sound like a normal person. Because I am. I'm not posh, I don't put on airs and graces. All I do, really, is say what we're all thinking. That's it. But to the media, that's bloody refreshing. I think that's why there's been so much interest.'

I never talk about where I'm from. It doesn't really matter, does it? Specificity, and *lived experience*, that's for the others. The people who don't belong here. Relatability – universality – doesn't require details. I gesture broadly towards unspecified places and times, when things were somehow better. What matters is that it's not now, not London.

'That's all it is, Martin. Honesty. I say what I mean and people know where they stand. It's a rare quality these days.'

'Speaking of honesty . . . as we've been so frank this evening.' He readjusts himself in his seat, undeterred by its squeaking protest. 'There is one particular, ah, subject that you've remained remarkably quiet on . . .' He glances again at his sheet – feigned nervousness, I expect, intended to disarm me. 'But, well, given your recent . . . importance, shall we call it, within the public debate, we would all, I'm sure, appreciate some illumination of your particular . . . stance.'

Finally, after more of this painfully stilted preamble, his ludicrous hemming and hawing, he gets to the question. I won't repeat it. It's the sort of fruitlessly polarising topic that's basically radioactive in the modern discourse. Eager for my answer, he sticks his chin out with an air of challenge. It's an old, tired trick. But it works. However I respond, there'll be a juicy pull quote tomorrow, and the ensuing row in the papers and online will tarnish me, and raise his profile. Thing is, this sort of empty, angry 'debate' achieves nothing. Nothing constructive, anyway. Or even destructive. All it results in is empty-calorie engagement. The metrics tail wagging the content dog. I run my tongue along the top row of my teeth, then place the tumbler back down on the table. Finally, I angle my torso squarely at Martin.

Not today, fuckface.

'You wouldn't ask a man that question. No, come on now—' I flash up a firm palm, staving away any interruption. 'You wouldn't. I'm not one to cry sexism, but I do need to call bullshit here. Look, you're young, you're keen. I understand that. You want a splashy scoop from this interview to write up in your little magazine. But I'm going to deprive you of that tonight. Alright? Okay, good. Don't pout.' Leaning back, expansively, I direct my attention to the muted audience. 'Energy bills have been unaffordable for months now. Working families – the people we as journalists owe the most to – haven't been able to make ends meet. It might not seem like that from *Perspective!*'s fancy London office, with your espresso machines and coconut water and whatever else. But that's the truth of it. So instead of rehashing online debates, let's talk. Let's actually have a proper conversation about the things that matter to everyday Britons. Real problems, real solutions.'

153

Age helps, in a manoeuvre like this. Delivery is everything. With the exasperated disappointment of a teacher, I've managed to completely release his pressure and sidestep the question. He shuffles again through his stack of papers, with less ease this time. More panic. Knees pressed together now, he's almost folded in on himself, no longer sprawling all over the stage.

'So let's pretend you didn't cock that up, Marty. Fresh start. We've got' – I look down at the clock – 'five or so minutes left. What would you like to ask me?'

I offer a lukewarm smile of encouragement. Rumbling builds within the audience as we wait for what he'll say.

'Er, I . . . ahm.' He blinks, and looks around. Stunned. The shock of my rebuke seems to have winded him. He was expecting an easy win against me, no doubt. 'I, well, ah . . .'

A few sheets fall from his lap. He watches their whispering descent. I feel suddenly, viciously, bored. Without even knowing that I'm doing it, not really, I find that I'm leaning over to him, jeering: '*Er, er, er . . . um, um, um . . .*' My voice is high-pitched and throaty, a cruel imitation of his stammer. I drop back to my usual low register and bark, 'Come on now, spit it out! We don't have all *er, um, er er* night.'

The young interviewer looks to me – naked hurt in his eyes. It was too far, too nasty. The room is absolutely silent. I succumbed to an impulse that I usually keep in check, only allowed out through the safe medium of a keyboard and word processor. His face falls blank. I wonder, and I can't deny that the thought amuses me, whether or not he'll actually *cry*. This is the guy I was warned about? This idiot? A loud snort escapes me, and then it happens. I don't – can't – hide it. I throw my head back and roar with laughter.

What else could the poor sod do? He tries to laugh along, gamely. Offers the nervy audience an apologetic shrug. Rather than reattempt speech, he reaches forward, over his papery lap, for the water. The carafe, frosted with condensation, slips dangerously from his grasping fingers. But he manages to get a hold of it and pour without incident. Calmer now, I sip my whisky again, watching as he gulps the water down.

'That's . . . that's better,' he says, after setting the empty glass back on the table. With a tight fist in front of his mouth, he gives a throaty cough.

'Clock's ticking . . .' I nudge him along. 'Do you have a final question for me?'

'Right, ah, okay,' he says, then clasps his palms together and breathes in. I can see the gleam of sweat across his flushed forehead and cheeks.

'You're a . . . a formidable woman, Lenny. Some would even say you're on a warpath.' He pauses there, as if expecting a challenge or a chuckle, though neither comes, and soon he picks up again. 'But I'm interested in what's beneath that steely exterior. Could you tell us, Lenny, what motivates you? What does *Lenny's vision of the future* look like? What are you, erm, fighting for?'

I could have answered that, once.

I feel so old sometimes. So tired. But it's not a scary or disappointing feeling. In fact, it's a relief. The lion's share of my life is behind me. Good riddance. I don't want to see how all this ends. I've grown so disgusted by this world, all of the idiot-people who inhabit it and the ugly things they do, and say, the smallness of their minds and lives and thoughts. Their barely conscious reward-seeking behaviour is so predictable. So suggestible. In aggregate, this infinite smallness amounts to a force so great, so overwhelming, that I cannot see beyond it. It's all I can do to not become a part of it. Not to become stupefied myself. What is there to hope for? Fight for?

I lift my glass high, then smile sweetly upwards, into the darkness. To the five hundred apparent faces looking to me for answers or entertainment or meaning. I can't make out any human forms from here, where I sit, illuminated on the centre stage. Maybe there aren't any. Maybe I'm the only real person in the world.

I tilt the glass forward, DiCaprio's Gatsby.

'Simple,' I tell my audience.

And I mean it. That's the key to all this: whenever I need to, I really do mean it.

'I'm fighting for you.'